French Kiss
DIARY ♥F
A CRUSH

By Sarra Manning

Adorkable
Nobody's Girl
Guitar Girl
Let's Get Lost
Pretty Things
Fashionistas series

Diary of a Crush series
French Kiss
Kiss and Make Up
Sealed With a Kiss

French Kiss

DIARY 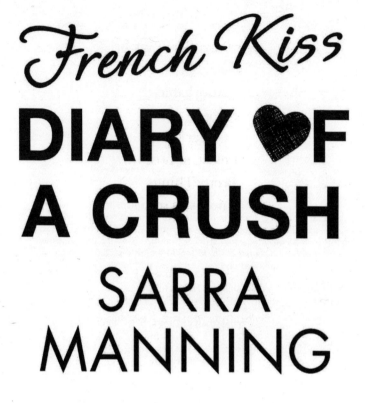OF
A CRUSH
SARRA
MANNING

www.atombooks.net

ATOM

Written by Sarra Manning and based on
the *J17* column *Diary of a Crush*

First published in Great Britain in 2004 by Hodder Children's Books
This paperback edition published in 2013 by Atom
Reprinted 2013

A CIP catalogue record for this book
is available from the British Library.

ISBN 978-0-349-00156-2

Printed and bound in Great Britain by
Clays Ltd, St Ives plc

Papers used by Atom are from well-managed forests
and other responsible sources.

MIX
Paper from
responsible sources
FSC® C104740

Atom
An imprint of
Little, Brown Book Group
100 Victoria Embankment
London EC4Y 0DY

An Hachette UK Company
www.hachette.co.uk

www.atombooks.net

Acknowledgements

Thanks to Ally Oliver, my editor at *J17*, who commissioned me to write the *Diary of a Crush* as a monthly column and her successor, Sophie Wilson, for continuing to commission me to write *Diary of a Crush*.

I would also like to thank Emily Thomas for giving me my first proper book deal after reading *Diary of a Crush*, my agent Karolina Sutton for working so hard and tirelessly on my behalf and Samantha Smith, Kate Agar and all at Atom for giving these books a shiny, new home.

Finally, I'd like to thank all the readers of *Diary of a Crush*. From the *J17* days, to the people who bought the books first time round, to you (yes YOU!) discovering Dylan and Edie for the first time. What a long, strange trip it's been.

Dedicated to the late, great, never out of date Gordon and Regina Shaw, who put up with me when I was a teenager.

Manchester Diary One: September – March

TOTALLY PRIVATE!!!

Name: Edie Wheeler
Age: Sixteen
Lives: Manchester via Brighton
Height: 160 cm
Weight: Fifty-eight to sixty-eight kg (depending on how much ice cream I've eaten in a twenty-four-hour period)
Hair: Getting blonder with every application of Clairol Golden Apricot
Eyes: Blue
Favourite book: *Emma* by Jane Austen
Favourite film: *Whip It*, *Toy Story 2* and *Breakfast at Tiffany's* (it's impossible to pick just one)
Favourite TV show: Oh, *X Factor*, I wish I could quit you
Lust objects: Ryan Gosling, Dean Speed from The Hormones and Dylan
Girl hero: Zooey Deschanel

Favourite website: www.hellogiggles.com
Favourite thing in the world: My vintage Dior handbag
I bought off eBay
Make-up item I couldn't live without: At least 3 bottles
of nail polish about my person at any one time
Ambition: For Dylan to fall wildly and passionately in
love with me and take me on a roadtrip across America

14th September

Do you ever get the feeling that you're waiting for your life to begin? I feel like I invented that feeling. 'Cause today is all about shiny, new things. Scary, shiny new things. And instead of jumping out of bed, ready to dazzle the world with my brightest smile and my cute new hairslides, I'm huddled under my duvet, scribbling in my new Cath Kidston notebook.

I mean, I *should* be rising to the challenge but, y'know, not so much. It's my first day at college so, officially, I'm not a schoolgirl any more. And, OK, I might be doing A-levels but I'm doing 'em at a college where there are art students and drama students and everyone (apart from the savage, psycho Barbies studying Hairdressing who laughed at me in the canteen on the day I had my interview) is achingly cool.

So, how come I know that I'm going to feel so young and phoney compared to everyone else? Like, someone's going to tap me on the shoulder and say, 'Hey kid, you don't belong here, back to school.' But school and my friends are miles and miles away. Why did Dad have to get a new job and decide to transfer me, Mum and Pudding halfway across the country? Because he's hellbent on ruining my life and destroying what little self-esteem I have, that's why.

Did my heart love till now?

22nd September

I got this massive lecture from the parents at breakfast about 'making more of an effort to fit in' and 'we know the move was hard on you but it's been four weeks and you should have adjusted by now'. I'm sure they've taken lessons in how to make me feel like a socially dysfunctional freak of nature. They don't understand though. All the people in my classes at college were at school/youth club/Brownies together and they just *completely* ignore me. And, besides, it's really hard to just crowbar myself into other people's conversation, like, 'Me too! I love The Vaccines. Isn't the lead singer just the dreamiest?' Insert retching noises.

But I knew I wouldn't hear the end of this (my mother is the missing link between Rottweilers and rat-catchers) so I got pro-active and signed up for a Photography course that starts next week. I might not make any friends but at least I'll learn how to take arty, grainy black 'n' white shots of dead trees and stuff.

So, directly after scribbling my name onto the sign-up sheet on the noticeboard, I was ambling down the corridor, nothing on my mind but whether I should have another packet of Skips, when five minutes later my entire life changed! One moment it sucked and then the next, nothing was going to be the same again. No warning, no booming music. There I was in the canteen scraping a plastic stirry thing through the hot-chocolate granules at the bottom of my cup and hoping no-one would notice me sitting there all alone, when I looked up, locked into a pair of deep blue eyes, and felt my spiritual self shift into orbit.

His face was all hard planes and angles, cheekbones and jawline softened only by these pillowy lips. His hair was equally confused and couldn't decide whether it was a fin or a mullet or just really messy or all of the above. But it was the colour of liquorice, or maybe that really dark chocolate that I can only eat in tiny amounts because it's too rich. He was wearing jeans that were faded on the knees and dark blue everywhere else, a striped shirt and a suit jacket. All of him was in chaos and it was hard to work out whether he was beautifully odd or oddly beautiful. I never knew boys could be beautiful but this one was.

Then he kinda looked beyond me and frowned as if he was annoyed at my audacity for daring to be in his line of vision. Boys that look like that always reckon they can get away with that kind of behaviour. He's probably an arrogant dickweed but he's a drop-dead gorgeous, arrogant dickweed.

I saw him again, later that afternoon, striding across the college lawn like the hounds of hell were snapping at his heels. It was like everything around him slowed down and then I heard someone shout, 'Dylan!' and he turned round. His name's Dylan. Of course he's called Dylan. How could he be called anything else?

25th September

This is what I've found out about Dylan, or the heir to my heart, as I now think of him:

- He's on the Art Foundation course, and he's 19. He's three years older than me. Age gaps are very sexy.
- That means he's done his A-levels already.
- He's one of the in-crowd, along with his two friends: Paul (bleached streaks, old-skool trainers) and Simon (really tall, goatee-d, always wears a black turtle-neck).
- They spend a large part of each day in the café across the road, but upstairs, which apparently is far more socially acceptable than downstairs with all the housewives.
- Dylan works in Rhythm Records on Wednesday afternoons and all day Saturday.

How do I know all this? Because, I was incredibly brave today and actually spoke to this girl, called Mia, on my course.

I was sitting in our English class with an empty desk on the other side of me and an animated, 'I'm just waiting for all fifty of my closest friends to suddenly materialise' expression on my face, when she plonked herself down next to me.

I glanced at her but she was rummaging about in

her bag so I went back to doodling Dylan's name all over my notebook.

'I like your nail varnish.'

No-one has ever spoken to me at college apart from the teachers, so it took me a moment to process the information that she was actually talking. To me. I looked at a sparkly red nail and then at her. She gave me a look like she thought I was possibly mentally challenged.

'Um, thanks. I didn't realise you were speaking to me,' I muttered.

She nodded impatiently. 'So, are you from Manchester Girls' School? I don't recognise you.'

It was strange. Like, she wasn't actually being rude but there was something in her tone of voice that wasn't far off it.

'No, I'm from Brighton,' I said, and I've never been more aware of my posh southern accent. 'My dad got transferred here over the summer. My name's Edie.'

'Eddie?'

'No, Edie. It's short for Edith.' I mumbled the last bit because I hate the evil joke that my parents decided to put on my birth certificate.

'I'm Mia,' the girl announced. 'I was named after this actress called Mia Farrow.'

'It's a cool name,' I ventured nervously because it was, and after a moment's pause, Mia smiled at me.

'Thanks. So do you like living here?'

'It's all right,' I said without much conviction. 'I miss my friends though.'

Mia nodded and then glanced over at my notebook, which was lying on the desk with Dylan's name plastered all over it.

'Oh, Dylan,' she grinned knowingly. 'He's very snackable. When did you meet him?'

My face went exactly the same shade as my nail varnish and I stuttered some nonsense about how Dylan was actually the name of a guy from Brighton but Mia wasn't buying it for a second.

'Yeah, right,' she snorted. 'Everyone loves Dylan. It's like a rite of passage thing. You get breasts, you realise that sitting downstairs in Fritzsch's is terminally uncool and you fall in love with Dylan.'

'Are you in love with Dylan then?' Just by saying his name, it felt like I'd signed my soul over to the devil.

Mia snorted again. 'No, because I'm in love with his best friend, Paul. He's in love with me too. We're a regular love fest.'

And then she went into this long, complicated story about Paul and his ex-girlfriend that I couldn't really follow but I nodded a lot and then I tried to make a few discreet enquiries about Dylan but I might just as well have had 'I fancy Dylan' tattooed on my forehead. Yeah, that's how subtle I am.

30th September

Dylan sat at the table in front of me today in the canteen, but, like, facing me. I pretended to be engrossed in one of my English books but I couldn't help stealing these glances at him. His left eyebrow is broken by a scar, a thin white line; it made me feel weird every time I looked at it. I wonder how it happened.

I think he was copying someone's homework (do Foundation Art students get homework?) because he sat all hunched over a pile of papers and an A4 pad, a pen clenched in his long fingers, and his forehead all crinkled up, like he was deep in thought.

It made me feel sad because even though he was just a couple of metres away from me, he was really a million miles out of my reach. He was beautiful and everyone loved him and there I was sharing breathing space with him and he didn't even know I existed.

I felt small and insignificant. He was a proper person. I was just a stupid kid.

He probably didn't trip up the bus stairs regularly or lose all his cognitive thought processes when he was in close proximity to someone he fancied. Oh, please don't let him fancy anyone!

And then he looked up. And his face came to life as this girl sashayed over to him and planted a kiss on his cheek. A pretty, hipster girl with an inky black bob and a slash of crimson lipstick and a cute black mini-dress, which would have looked ridiculous on me.

That would be Shona, Paul's infamous ex-girlfriend. Mia told me all about her yesterday. Apparently her and Dylan have been friends ever since they bonded in a sandpit at nursery school and they practically grew up together. So, that would make them like brother and sister, but I've never seen any siblings lovin' it up like they were. She was playing with his hair and he was JUST LETTING HER.

And the other suckiness that was my day? The people in my English class hate me. They were sitting on the next table along from me in the café and talking about how I was 'up myself' and 'weird'. Better than being a bunch of cookie-cutter deadheads.

4th October

I'm just back from a weekend in Brighton, staying with the grand'rents and hanging out with my old friends. It's only been a month since I last saw them but everything seemed different. Toby and Alice are now going out, which just amazes me because I can still remember the time we were rehearsing the Nativity play at infant school and he wet himself and then pulled baby Jesus' crib over the puddle. Alice is snogging him on a regular basis! Tish has dyed her hair pink. Eve's parents are splitting up. I can't believe how much happens in such a short space of time. They were all talking about sixth-form college and having long conversations about people I didn't know and though they made a big effort to include me, I felt like I was being left behind. I know what will happen. The phone calls and the emails and the monthly visits will all tail off and, eventually, we'll lose contact. So I won't have any friends left there and I certainly don't have any friends here.

7th October

I couldn't write last night because my hands were still shaking! Picture the scene: me skulking into that stupid Photography course in my skinny jeans that sag at the knees and a scruffy old black T-shirt 'cause I couldn't be arsed to make any effort and then I nearly fall out of my Converses because who's taking up the back row but Dylan! And Paul! And Simon! In fact, the whole class was full of art students (apparently they have to take it as part of their course), so Martyn (the tutor) told me to sit in the back row next to Paul as there was nowhere else to sit.

It was the most exquisite torture. Paul sort of smiled at me but my face had contorted into this weird grimace. And then Dylan leaned across Paul and spoke to me.

'Hey,' he said in this voice that was all broken glass and silk. 'Have you got a spare pen I can borrow?'

I am the lamest girl in the world. All I could do was

shake my head. My tongue had become this heavy, lumpy thing. But when I got my camera out (a 'sorry for ruining your life' present from Dad) I heard him say to Simon, 'She's got a cool camera!'

The photography lesson went straight over my head. I couldn't take my eyes off Dylan's hands. He's got beautiful fingers; they're really long and thin and look like they should be permanently picking out chords on a shiny, red gee-tar. Also, when the class was over, they all went out for coffee but he held the door open for me and WINKED at me! I can't believe that my stomach lurched at such obvious behaviour but, hey, it did. My *everything* lurched.

13th October

College has been a lot better. I get on really well with Mia. Well, she goes on and on about Paul (she's made me tell her, like, fifty times about sitting next to him in Photography) and I've started hanging out with these two boys, Nat and Trent, from my History of Art class. They're really cool. Nat has the naughtiest expression on his face all the time, like he's thinking evil things. And Trent is so pint-sized and cute that I want to pick him up and stash him in my pencil case and take him home. They came over to talk to me when they saw the Rookiemag.com sticker on my folder and said that they'd seen me around and had been daring each other to come and say hello.

'Why didn't you just come over and say hi?' I asked them. And Nat just shrugged and said that they were a bit intimidated by me, which is so wrong because I am the least intimidating person in the world. I mean, fluffy little baby bunny rabbits are more intimidating than me.

But the best thing that's happened is that Dylan is now actively aware of my existence! He smiles at me when he sees me. I can't believe I'm being such a wuss over a mere boy-shape, I seem to be losing all my kick-ass faculties.

In fact, everything was swimming along quite pleasantly and then life suddenly got seriously heavy and weird. When I got to Photography class yesterday (late as usual, but I had made a special effort and put on my favourite polka dot vintage dress and my new pink Converses), the only seat free was next to Dylan.

I felt as if all the molecules in my body were straining towards him. He was wearing a faded Coca-Cola T-shirt that had these little holes in it, like it was really old. And I realised that if I leaned very slightly to my right, his bare arm would be touching my bare arm, which made me feel almost sick with nerves.

I didn't even dare sneak any sideways looks at him but then Martyn said we had to get into pairs to do this assignment and told us to work with the people next to us. Yup, the impossible just fell right into my lap –

Dylan's my photographic partner! But instead of being pleased, it just made me want to cry.

I couldn't speak at all. I had to hide my hands under the table so he wouldn't see them shaking as he tried to talk to me.

'So I guess we haven't been formally introduced,' he said, and he looked at me, and all I could do was stare at my notebook on the table in front of me and know that every part of me was blushing. My face, the tips of my ears, even the bits between my toes. Dylan soldiered on. 'I'm Dylan, I'm on the Foundation Art course, are you doing A-levels?'

I managed to shake my head and shrug and nod in reply to all his questions. Give it a week or two and I might upgrade to the odd grunting noise.

Dylan had to decide what our project was going to be – which was taking photographs of lots of crumbling buildings, as far as I can tell. He was chattering away about the influence of the Gothic Revival in a lot of Manchester's architecture from the nineteenth century and I could barely hear him, though he did say something about 'flying buttresses' and then laughed.

I think it's fair to say that Dylan's got me down as a mute. Even worse, he's coming here, TO MY HOUSE on Sunday. This is not a good thing, especially as I actually had to talk to him at that point and try to be cool and not forget my address. I started stammering and blushing even more than I already had. It was hideous. And I glanced up and he was just giving me this look accompanied by a little half-smile that just about removed the top layer of my skin.

15th October

I can't concentrate on anything but the fact that Dylan is coming over on Sunday. By some miracle, the 'rents are going to a wedding on Saturday and staying over so they won't be home until Sunday night late and my mother won't be barging in, proffering Ribena and oatcakes.

Mia told me that Dylan has a terrible rep and that he's left a 'trail of broken hearts in every girls' school from here to Cheshire'. And that he and Shona have this strange contest to see who can get off with the most people but it's really because they have this love/hate relationship and they're trying to score points off each other.

'Mia, have you *seen* Dylan?' I asked her incredulously as we sat on the wall by the Nursery Block and split a bag of chips between classes. 'He's gorgeous. If he wanted Shona, he could have her. He doesn't need to play games.'

But Mia just gave me a funny look and then changed the subject.

I can't seem to settle. I wish Sunday was here and then I wish that it was never, ever going to happen. When I'm alone inside my head, I have these amazing conversations with Dylan and I'm funny and intelligent and just a little bit quirky. But in reality I know that I'm too chicken to even speak to him.

17th October
In twenty-four hours Dylan will be in my house. It's just too awful to contemplate. And if I wasn't stressed enough, Mia's invited herself to stay over tonight. I like her and all, but I just wanted to be alone tonight so I could work myself up into a hysterical state.

18th October
Mia's as good as dead. She came around, spiked my Diet Pepsi with vodka and then persuaded me that it'd be a really good idea to cut a fringe in. 'You've got really cool eyebrows, but no-one can see 'em,' she kept saying. And I felt so woozy that in the end she just kind of lunged at me with the scissors and butchered my hair. *Then* she threw up on my mum's Art Deco rug.

Dylan's coming round in half an hour. The lounge stinks of Dettol, I've got a killer headache and worst of all, my so-called fringe is crooked and curling up at the ends. I wish I was dead. No I don't – I wish everyone else was dead.

18th October (later)
By the time Dylan actually turned up I was practically hyper-ventilating. Every time I looked in the mirror my

fringe had become even more lame. It was flicking out at the edges and just wouldn't lie flat. Did I mention that it was completely uneven too?

I was just in the middle of changing, so I was wearing my new dark denim skirt *and* the Lisa Simpson T-shirt I'd slept in, when the doorbell rang. I swear to God, my limbs went into spasms. I managed to open the door and Dylan was slouched nonchalantly (my word for the week) against the door jamb, dressed all in black. He slowly uncoiled himself, smiled at me in a not very reassuring way and handed me a carrier bag. 'I thought we could have these with our tea,' he said, with another smile that was a millimetre away from being a smirk.

I just stared at my feet, but eventually I took the bag and looked inside.

He'd brought biscuits. When I glanced at him, he was staring at me really intently. It was my *bloody* fringe, wasn't it?

'You look different,' he said after I'd just stood there and gazed at him for five minutes. Then, he reached out his hand and lifted my chin. My stomach dipped all the way down to the silver nail varnish on my toes. I pulled away 'cause I just couldn't bear it any longer.

'It's my fringe. I had a run-in with a pair of scissors,' I muttered and he was like, 'Wow, you actually talk!'

And then we were sitting on the stairs and I told

him about Mia and he said in this strange, strained voice, 'Oh, that sounds like Mia.'

I looked at our knees and mine just looked so small and childish compared to his. Even his knees seem dangerous. Does that sound strange?

Anyway, to cut a long story short, quite literally, we ended up in the bathroom so that Dylan could tidy up my fringe. He was really into the idea and I figured that it couldn't look any worse.

It was a very, very intimate situation. I sat on the edge of the tub and Dylan knelt in front of me, cupping my chin and turning my head this way and that before he started snipping. I'd always vaguely thought that all boys who cut hair had to be gay – but Dylan seemed so not gay. The way he went about cutting my fringe was more about me being a sculpture or a drawing and him being an artist, moulding clay or smudging charcoal.

And then when he'd finished, he wouldn't let me look. Instead he did something which freaked me out. He told me to close my eyes and he started, very gently, blowing on my face to get rid of all the icky little hairs. He was holding me by the shoulders to stop me from moving and I wanted him to kiss me so badly. More than I've ever wanted anything.

But he didn't.

He just turned me round to face the mirror and I have to admit my hair was happening. My fringe was really,

really short but it suited me. That devastating half-smile which makes me turn into a puddle of not-quite-set jelly was back on Dylan's face again but he just said, 'I've given you a 1960s urchin cut. It looks really cute.'

I was sort of 'aw shucks'-ing but he just said dead seriously, 'Your eyebrows are fantastic.' Then the moment was gone, so I went downstairs and made him some tea.

But the kettle had barely boiled before Dylan had to go. It was just, 'Time I wasn't here.' We didn't even take any photos or talk. One moment he was in the kitchen dunking digestives into his tea and I was summoning up the courage to open my mouth and form complete sentences, the next he was out the front door. He didn't even say goodbye. I watched him disappear down the street and as he got further and further away, the sadder I felt. Then I realised the 'rents would be home any minute so I went to inspect the rug for puke damage.

Later on, I googled 60s urchin cuts and there were lots of pictures of girls with a mod-look who were all very pretty in a really gamine way.

I wondered if Dylan thought I was pretty in a gamine way . . . or was it just my fringe?

I have to stop this obsessing about him but it's almost like I want to consume Dylan whole. When I'm with him, I'm a different person. I become really aware of myself and I'm not sure I like it. I don't know. Why is this whole boy/girl thing so confusing?

19th October

I felt dreadful today, like I had this sense of impending doom hanging over me. I spent most of the night thinking about what had happened with Dylan. And I also remembered how unimpressed he was with Mia. I didn't see Dylan at all, but I saw his friend, Paul, who smiled at me. Not in a sleazy way, more in a friendly way. I also saw Mia who I thought might apologise for puking on my mum's rug. But she just sneered at me and said, 'Your fringe is ridiculously short.' And I said, 'Well, whose fault is that?' Then she muttered something under her breath about girls with stupid crushes and how I should just get a life. So, then I was like, 'Oh yeah, I had a great time with Dylan on Sunday in case you were interested and Paul's just smiled at me.' She kind of shoved me against the wall and then stormed off.

But Nat and Trent said that I looked a little bit like Emma Watson and I beamed at them, because that was so the right thing to say.

20th October

I sat in the canteen on my own and Mia sat nearby with a bunch of people who kept looking over at me and laughing. Then, if that wasn't bad enough, Dylan walked in with Shona and even though there were two spare seats on my table, they sat as far away as possible.

Shona is gorgeous. She looks like she's stepped out

of the pages of a style mag or something. She wears the same stuff as me (jeans and little cardies or vintage dresses) but she looks a million times better. I was so conscious of my bottle-green, school cardie and boring black cords. Sometimes a girl just can't pull off the casual thang.

Anyway, they just locked into this private groove, whispering and giggling softly. Dylan had his arm round her and every now and again she'd sort of nuzzle her head against his shoulder. I pretended that I was engrossed in my book, but I just sat there and wondered why the sound of people laughing could be, like, the loneliest sound in the world. Then Dylan got up and as he passed me he tugged one of my pigtails, but he'd gone before I could turn round. I watched Shona from behind my book and she was writing really fast and feverishly. Reams of it.

When it was time to go, she tore up what she'd been writing, chucked all the little bits of paper in the bin and wafted past me. Our eyes met for a second, so I tried to smile but she stuck her nose in the air and marched out. Everything was so weird. Why was Mia being such a bitch? And why was Dylan avoiding me? And why did Shona get to be beautiful and mysterious in such a cool way?

No Photography today as Martyn's off sick. Can't decide if I'm disappointed or relieved with all the stuff that's going on.

23rd October

Nat and Trent are the only people speaking to me, apart from the 'rents who don't count. Obviously, I'm a horrible person and no-one wants to know me.

I saw Dylan in town. He was with Shona. Again. He seemed so remote – I realised it was stupid to imagine that there was some bond between us. When I see him tomorrow, I'm going to pretend that he doesn't exist. It's about the only way that I can hold on to my last shreds of sanity.

27th October

Oh God, I've made such a fool of myself. I'm sitting in the naff café that no-one ever goes into and I've got to go to Photography class in a minute but I'm not sure that I can.

My obsession with Dylan has leaked over into an obsession with Shona. They're always whispering together lately and I know there's all sorts of secrets going on and it's driving me crazy. I'm sure there's more to this 'best friends since we were embryos' thing.

This morning I walked into the first floor loos to hear Shona screeching at Mia, 'Just keep your stinking carcass away from him!' before storming out. Then Mia shot me an absolutely filthy look before disappearing. I'm getting so fixated on Shona that I even followed her at morning break. She went into Oxfam and I hid behind the book-stand and watched her nearly buy this really cool Sixties black bag. So, I bought it instead, when she'd left. I'm practically stalking her.

It got worse. At afternoon break, she sat in the library doing her manic scribbling routine again and then chucking it all in the bin. Five minutes later (when I should have been in French), I was rifling through the bin and hoping that there wasn't any goopy stuff in there when I felt two hands squeeze my waist.

I turned my head, dead flustered, and Dylan was standing right behind me, smiling and saying, 'What on earth are you doing, weirdo? Did you miss breakfast or something?' A million things were running through my head. Did he know what I was really up to? Why was he always laughing at me? I was trembling like a leaf in a thunderstorm. I could feel his warm breath on the top of my head and his hands resting on my waist, seemed really cool while my skin burned up.

I leaned back against him for one second and he lowered his head like, I don't know, like he was about to kiss me. But it was just all too much, I twisted away from him and shot out of the library.

How can I ever face him again?

27th October (later)
By the time I got to Photography class, there was nowhere to sit but in the back row with Simon, Paul

and . . . Dylan. Which is getting to become something of a habit. Note to self: Get to Photography class ON TIME! I couldn't even look at Dylan, so I just pretended that he wasn't there even though I could sense him looking at me in this bemused fashion. I turned round and scowled at him. 'Stop staring at me!'

Dylan seemed to think that was hugely funny 'cause he smirked, 'Well, stop sulking then.'

I was just about to deny it, when Martyn, our tutor, told us to get into our project pairs and discuss our work, so I had to talk to Dylan. After a couple of moments of trying to stare each other out, I gave in and started wittering on about the photographs.

'So, um, I don't really know where there would be any crumbly old houses . . . that is, I mean, y'know, stuff that's old and Gothicky Revivaly 'cause I've only just moved here.' I went on like that for ages. I could hear myself talking all this utter crap and tried telling myself to shut up but myself wouldn't listen and all the while Dylan sat there and stared at me. Like, really stared at me. It made me feel really uncomfortable, but sort of excited at the same time.

I was going round in circles, so Dylan decided to take charge. 'There's this old ruined abbey halfway to the moors that we should go to,' he announced suddenly, sitting up straight. 'You'll love it, it's all Gothicky Revivaly.' He shot me a slightly evil smile and yay me because I managed to roll my eyes rather than do what I normally do which is turn bright red and start hyper-ventilating.

'OK, whatever,' I mumbled.

'I've got to work on Saturday so let's do it Sunday week,' Dylan continued. He was being very take charge, which was quite impressive. If I have to organise a cinema outing, it usually takes me at least a day to decide what film to see. 'I'll come round to yours for about one and then we can drive up there,' he said.

All I could think about was that Dylan was going to drive me, *in his car*, to an old, ruined abbey a few miles out of town. I'm going to be trapped in a small, enclosed space with Dylan for at least an hour each way.

When Dylan and I walked out of the classroom, Shona was waiting for him. It was very awkward. Dylan suddenly grabbed my hand as I was about to scurry away, which startled me and made me crash into the wall, and he said, 'Shona, Edie. Edie, Shona.' Shona gave me this really pointed look and said very icily, 'Yes, I know.'

What the hell is going on?

28th October
The weirdest day, ever. I didn't see Dylan, but I bumped into Shona in the Cancer Research shop. We both made a lunge for this gorgeous Sixties-ish dress

25

with cherries printed on it. Just as I was about to give it up and beg her not to hurt me, she smiled and said, 'Oh, this would look way better on you.'

I tried it on and it looked fab. I was really surprised to find Shona lurking around the till and I nearly fainted when she asked me to go for a coffee with her. Like, we were friends and she didn't mind being seen with a total geek girl. In the end I skipped French and spent the whole afternoon hanging with her. She asked me what I thought of Dylan's mates, Simon and Paul, but then she started pumping me for information on who Mia was dating. I told her all about Mia getting me drunk and how Dylan had rescued my fringe and she was like, 'Mia's the biggest bitch this side of the equator, keep away from her.'

I was sort of trying to find out whether Shona and Dylan had ever bumped uglies, but basically I was just going on and on about him in a really sad fashion. Shona wouldn't admit anything – she just smiled knowingly. Before we went our separate ways, she suddenly gripped my arm tightly and said, 'Don't get too besotted with Dylan, Edie. He eats up little girls like you for breakfast.'

Was that friendly advice or a warning to back the hell off?

31st October
Nat and Trent forced me to go trick or treating with

them. They decided to go as Jedward and I dressed up as a dead girl from a splatter movie.

So there I was tramping the streets covered in fake blood with a rubber pick-axe stuck to my back. The carrier bag of chocolate we'd got was almost worth it, until I saw Dylan and a huge bunch of his mates (well, like, five of them) coming towards us. THERE WAS NOWHERE TO HIDE!!! I ran across two busy lanes of traffic and nearly succeeded in getting mown down by a bus and replacing my fake blood with a couple of pints of the real thing.

Nat and Trent told me I hadn't got away with it anyway. They'd heard Dylan say, 'Someone's parents never taught her to look both ways when she's crossing the road.' Oh God. Oh God. Oh God.

Nat and Trent were like, 'Time to engage the brain cell,' but I think I looked so desolate that they finally stopped teasing me (which they'd done mercilessly for about half an hour) and shared their chocolate with me instead.

2nd November
When I went to get some books out of my locker at lunchtime, I found a note from Shona asking me if I wanted to go to a gig with her next week and to give her a ring.

I went swimming at lunchtime and afterwards, as I hurried out of the sports centre, I bumped into Dylan.

When I say bumped, I actually mean that I hurtled into him with all the velocity of a high-speed train. I had Tinie Tempah on my iPod and he always makes me walk really, really fast. Dylan put his hands out to steady me and I could feel them through my T-shirt. I had wet hair and tatty old trackie bottoms on, why couldn't he see me when I looked less dorkish?

'I've been swimming,' I said, as if he couldn't already tell. Dylan still had his hands on my shoulders and he sort of gently pushed me against the wall and bent his head, so his lips were almost touching mine and whispered, 'We've got a date on Sunday. See you then, kid.' And off he sauntered.

Although I'm really into Dylan, I hate the way that he treats me like his little personal plaything. I think he must know that I fancy him, which is horrible enough, but why does he have to make me feel so lame about it?

8th November

I'm thawing out in front of the fire with a mug of hot choc and a headful of strange thoughts.

Dylan picked me up this lunchtime in this tiny bashed-up car. I had to sit with my knees hunched against the dashboard because my seat wouldn't go back and when Dylan got in it seemed even more cramped. Our eyes met in the driver's mirror and we both smiled. Time seemed to get really slow and then stop altogether.

He said, 'It's OK, Edie. I know,' (which I think is the first time he's ever said my name and just confirmed my worst fears that he'd guessed I had a planet-sized crush on him) before putting on a Beatles CD and starting the car.

I never wanted the journey to end. Occasionally Dylan's hand would brush my leg as he changed gears but it wasn't sleazy, it didn't even make my heart skip a couple of beats, it just felt really, well, *right*. I sunk as far as I could into the seat and listened to the music and the car purring along the country roads. Dylan and I were silent but it wasn't awkward; it was, like, the most comfortable quiet in the world.

When we got there, wherever *there* was – I didn't have a clue – I had to scramble over the driver's seat, because he'd parked against a hedge. Dylan just stood there while I tried not to snag my woolly tights. I wished I hadn't worn a dress.

'You could've helped me,' I muttered.

Dylan just grinned. 'You seemed to manage very well all by yourself.'

'Charming,' I said witheringly, but you could tell I didn't really mean it.

We had to scramble up this hill with, like, a force 10 gale blowing, so Dylan grabbed my hand and pulled me up behind him. The ruins were all twisty and pointy, a bit like Dylan. He was fiddling with my camera.

'You ready for your close-up then?' he asked with a

smile. There was no way I was going to let Dylan photograph me, I felt vulnerable enough. I snatched the camera back.

'No, I wanna take pictures of *you*. It's my camera.'

Dylan shrugged, then stood there glaring at me. 'Come on, then.'

He was ruining everything by going weird and moody. It made me feel very aggressive. I yanked him, so he was standing in a crumbling doorway and then shoved the camera lens towards his face and took photos as fast as I could. I surprise myself sometimes. Then he surprised me by pushing the camera away and kissing me.

I knew then that nothing else mattered because I wanted to die from Dylan's kisses. He did things to my mouth that made me realise what it was for. All the time I'd been using it to eat and talk and blow bubbles from wads of Hubba Bubba and instead its sole purpose in life was to be the place where Dylan's tongue stroked along my teeth and the insides of my cheeks and danced with mine.

I realise now that the way that someone kisses is as individual as the way they do their hair. Also, there's no right or wrong way to do it. It was a major revelation. When Dylan kissed me, I couldn't help but believe that I was the only girl in the world that he'd never get enough of and it made me fall a whole lot more in love with him.

His hands were in my hair and his lips were on mine and it was like everything and nothing that I'd expected. It seemed to last for ages before *he* pushed me away.

'That didn't happen,' he hissed, narrowing his eyes. 'Let's get out of here.'

On the way back down the hill to the car, I slipped and fell over. Dylan didn't even help me, he just watched impatiently while I scrambled to my feet. We drove back in this horrible silence and I couldn't get out of the car fast enough when we got to my house. He was already driving off before I'd even shut the door.

What the hell did I do wrong?

9th November

Dylan ignored me all day. As luck would have it, I kept bumping into him everywhere I went but it was like I was invisible; he just brushed past me like a sudden gust of cold air.

Shona kept pestering me about going to some gig tonight. She was really friendly and I wanted to ask her if she'd spoken to Dylan but I was too chicken.

I didn't feel like going out but Shona wouldn't take no for an answer. She came round to my house and lounged on my bed while I decided to wear my new dress with the cherries on it and a little red cardie. She's not at all scary now that I know her, but she *is* annoyingly tight-lipped about Dylan.

'So did Dylan say anything about me then?' I plucked up the courage to ask, after about ten minutes.

'No,' Shona replied flatly, flicking through my copy of *The Virgin Suicides*. 'Any reason why he should?'

I pretended to be doing my hair but really I wanted to look at Shona without her realising it. To see if she was twitching or something and therefore lying about Dylan not saying anything.

'Oh, it's just we went out the other afternoon to do this project and I thought he might have mentioned it,' I said ultra-casually but Shona just shrugged.

And when we got to the club, who do we see but Dylan with *Mia* all over him! Shona made a beeline for them, and I trailed (unwillingly) along behind her. She and Dylan started having this really quiet, really heated debate, while Mia looked me up and down with this really evil smirk on her face. I had to get away, she was doing my head in, so I got myself a drink and wandered off to watch the band, which is when I started talking to this skate kid. He kept telling me that I looked really fresh and I knew Dylan was watching me, so I smiled at this guy and touched his arm while he wittered on. Then skate kid grabbed me and shoved his tongue down my throat, which was so inappropriate and *ewwww* that it took a while to actually process what was happening. I pushed him away and told him to cut it out, just in time to see

Dylan looking at me with a disgusted expression on his face.

I didn't go and find Shona, I didn't even tell Dylan that he was a treacherous, two-faced git, I just shot out of the club, ran all the way home and collapsed on my bed.

10th November

I've been spending a lot of time hanging out with Nat and Trent (who *must* be gay. Or else they just really, really like show tunes). In fact, they're coming round to mine at the weekend for pizza and a Ryan Gosling DVD marathon. Shona asked why I hadn't stuck around to see the band last night and I was like, 'Some guy kept trying to suck face with me and wouldn't take no for an answer,' in the hope that she'd tell Dylan. But she just kept going on about what a witch Mia was.

I had Photography class in the afternoon. Dylan and I were meant to be developing the pictures we took but he obviously didn't want to be alone in a darkroom with me and we were chaperoned by Simon and Paul. Dylan slumped at the end of the bench glowering and talked to Simon in low murmurs (I distinctly heard the words 'she's a fucking headcase') while me and Paul actually managed to do the developing. I was glad it was dark. It's easier to hide your emotions when the lights are dim.

As Dylan's face emerged from the photographic

paper, I felt my insides turn to mush. His eyes seemed to look right through me and then I glanced at the real Dylan and it made me sad and angry that he couldn't even bring himself to look in my direction. Paul walked me to the top of my road. I don't fancy him, thank God, because one crush is about all I can handle, he's just very easy to talk to. But when I mentioned that I'd been hanging with Shona he went all quiet. And when I muttered something about Mia, he nearly tripped over his feet. I just don't understand boy-shapes.

16th November

I had a fantabulous time with Nat and Trent yesterday. I knew I was right about the gay thing because a) they insisted that we watch *The Notebook* twice! And b) they 'fessed all.

I'd just gone to get some more garlic bread out of the oven and when I came back they were all whispery but looked up immediately.

'Were you talking about me? Was it about me and Dylan?' I asked suspiciously because I have a one-track mind. Well, I have a several-track mind but they all go in the same Dylanwards direction.

I tapped my foot and glared at them while they nudged each other until Trent blurted out: 'We're gay. You know that, right?' And, honestly, they looked so scared like I was about to start screaming that I burst out laughing and said, 'Hey, what else is new?' It was all cool.

But today? Urgh! Mia and two of her hench-women cornered me in the loos.

'I want a word with you, you skanky slut,' were her first words. I almost dropped my make-up bag in the sink. WTF? 'Excuse me?' I said because I was too astounded to even be scared.

But Mia grabbed me by the wrist and slammed me right against the paper towel dispenser. 'You're such a ho,' she hissed. 'Everyone knows you've got off with Dylan *and* Paul.'

She was right in my face, practically spitting with venom and I felt all shaky and weepy 'cause when someone's nose to nose with you and giving you aggro, it's quite traumatising. Plus I didn't have a clue what she was going on about. I'd kissed Dylan. I'd had major kissing with Dylan and now he was treating me like a leper and as for Paul . . . Since when did walking home with someone equal letting them have a quick feel?

Luckily, a gang of secretarial trainees came in and she had to let me go but the whole thing left me very trembly.

I'd just about recovered and pushed the door open when I saw Shona walking down the corridor, and she blanked me! I thought that maybe she hadn't seen me and I ran and caught up with her.

'Hey you,' I said brightly and then took a step back as Shona shot me a venomous look. 'What's wrong?' I said.

'What's wrong? What's wrong?' she repeated with disbelief. 'What's wrong is that I've been hanging out with a two-faced bitch like you!' She flounced off in the direction of the art block and I went to another bathroom and sat on the toilet seat and cried until it was time for French. I think everyone must be on drugs. I don't know what's going on. It seemed like the whole college was pointing at me and whispering. To top it all, I saw Dylan on my way to the bus-stop and he looked at me like I'd just crawled out of a primordial swamp.

I got home and had a huge hissy fit at the 'rents about moving to this hideous town in the first place but it didn't really make me feel better.

22nd November

I used to love the weekends when we lived in Brighton. From Friday evening to Sunday night, I'd be out of the house and hanging with my friends. I was part of a gang of people that cared about me. This weekend, I barely came out of my room. I mostly slumped on the bed, cuddling Pudding until even she got bored and miaowed indignantly until I let her out.

I spent the whole weekend either moping, gazing at that stupid photo of Dylan or phoning Shona only to have my calls roll to voicemail. Yeah, right. I know that this icky mess is all Dylan's fault.

23rd November

I was definitely at the back of the queue when they were handing out common sense.

I'd spent so long having these confrontation fantasies in my head about exactly what I was going to say to Dylan that I completely forgot all the very good reasons (about 147 of them at the last count) why I shouldn't corner him in a deserted studio at lunchtime.

The really sarcastic little speech that I'd prepared flew out of my head and I screamed and swore at him. Oh sweet baby Jesus, I was a total harpy!

'You're just an arrogant jerk who thinks he can play around with my heart just for something to do,' was one of the not-so-highlights of it. I even stamped my foot a couple of times. The more angry I got, the more choked up and snotty-nosed I became while Dylan sat there looking utterly horrified. Then I burst into tears properly and ran out. Sometimes I think that I suffer from arrested mental development.

I made it as far as the patch of ground by the kitchens where the bins are, before Dylan caught up with me. One moment I was running as fast as I could, the next he'd grabbed me by the shoulders and hauled me round to face him. Of course, I was struggling and flailing about like someone had emptied a packet of itching powder into my knickers but then I became aware of how tightly Dylan was holding me and I went still.

'God, just stop it,' he said and his voice was all strained. 'Calm down.' And he was looking at me like he really cared about me and then he stroked one long finger down my hot face and I knew he was going to kiss me. I *knew* it. It was even better than before. We melted into each other. He kissed me so hard and so long that time seemed to freeze around us.

After that we went for a walk in the park *and he held my hand*. Really held it. And every now and again, he'd squeeze my fingers. It was primo hand-holding. But I was still really mad at him. And he said, 'Edie, there's all this complicated stuff going on that I need to clear up.'

So I asked, 'You mean, before we can be together?'

He crinkled his eyes at me like he was seeing me for the first time and then he muttered, 'I don't want you to get hurt.' People always say that when they're about to hurt you.

It was the hardest thing that I've ever done but I just said in a small, tight voice, 'Well, when you're done with all these games, maybe you'll let me know.' I turned and walked away and I forced myself not to look back.

I think I felt worse, if that was possible, after that. I wish I'd never come here. Nat and Trent are the only people who speak to me. Shona acts as if I'm an icky piece of ick she's found at the bottom of her bag. Even though I hear whispers, I walk the corridors with my head up and my shoulders straight, even though deep inside I'm cringing. But it's hard. It's really hard. It's *too* hard.

24th November

Nat and Trent had a fight today. Nat pinched the last chip from Trent's plate. Trent stormed off and Nat went all sulky. I walked him round the park and we talked about finding a cure for boy disease.

Eventually after I'd been banging on and on about you-know-who for half an hour at least, Nat said, 'Edie you've got to let it go.' But really he was telling me to let Dylan go and I just can't do that. Even though Dylan seems to carry a huge amount of emotional baggage around with him, I can't suddenly forget the feel of his kisses and those rare moments when we really seem to . . . *connect.*

Then, talk of the devil, Dylan walked past our park bench. He was wearing his scuffed-up suede jacket and jeans. He glanced at me and then quickly looked away like he didn't even know me. Which I am so sick of. Is that all it's ever going to be? That he kisses me senseless then ignores me?

I was going to bunk Photography but I bumped into Martyn. Luckily he wanted me to help him set up a slide projector and operate the clicker so I kept away from Dylan all lesson. But at the end, as I walked past him, he seized my wrist.

'I want a word with you,' he hissed.

'What?'

'Saw you getting cosy with Nat in the park,' he said, his face flushing.

'Why, are you jealous?' I had the guts to say, before tugging my arm away and walking off.

He has no right to start acting like he cares about what I do with my life.

25th November

Mum let me take the day off college so we could go to Selfridges in the Trafford Centre to pick up stuff for my newly-decorated room. We had a blazing row in soft furnishings 'cause she reckoned that the Cath Kidston shabby-chic cushions I wanted were too expensive. Then she got all weepy about me leaving home to go to university in, like, two years and let me choose this cool café for lunch. I was just investigating the inside of my jacket potato when all the hairs on the back of my neck prickled as if someone was watching me. I swivelled round to see Dylan staring at me from another table.

My mum was wittering on about something and Dylan lifted up his coffee cup and gave me an ironic salute. It was awful. Mum wouldn't shut up and I was terrified/desperate (still haven't decided which) for Dylan to come over. I persuaded her to let me go off for half an hour.

As I walked out of the door, I knew Dylan was following me. My heart was beating really fast as he drew level with me and pulled me into an alley. We both reached for each other and then we were kissing like it was the end of the world. By the time I pulled away my lips were sore.

'You're just a kiss slut,' he sneered and then walked off.

What a creep! I caught up with him and punched him on the shoulder so hard that I yowled and had to suck on my knuckles because they hurt. Dylan turned round and looked at me with that horrible smirky expression of his that I hate but it disappeared pretty quickly when I shouted, 'Stay the hell out of my life!' right in his face. And the weird thing is that for about five minutes I really meant it, but as I wandered off, all quivery and tearful, to M&S to find The Mothership, I was like, what was I thinking of?

26th November

I refused to go to college today. I just can't face Dylan because I'll want to kiss him. And I can't face Shona 'cause she doesn't want to be my friend any more. And I can't face Mia because she's a demon from the seventh layer of hell.

I had my 'teen angst, do not disturb' face on, so Mum didn't argue when I slumped in front of *Daybreak* and refused to budge.

27th November

Skived off college again. Mum asked if I was ill and I was just like, 'I don't want to talk about it.' But later her and Dad ganged up on me and I got the whole, 'You know you can talk to us about anything' routine. They've got to be joking.

30th November

I managed to muster the energy to go to college. It was either that or face another lecture. I wore all black because it matched my mood and walked around with a scowl on my face as if to say, 'OK, you losers, so you don't like me? So what?'

I saw Dylan sitting in the canteen with Simon and Paul. I sat with my back to him, so I wasn't even tempted to look. Then the strangest thing happened. Mia suddenly plonked herself down next to me and started chatting as if we were the best of friends. I was so shocked I could barely speak. She was blathering on about some band that were playing on the weekend when I interrupted her. 'Uh, last time I saw you, you practically tried to beat me up.'

She didn't bat an eyelid. 'I was only mucking about. Anyway I heard on the vine that you and Dylan were finished.'

I smiled sweetly even though I felt like throttling her. 'And who said we ever got started?'

'But I thought . . .' Hah! That took the smarmy smile off her face.

'A few sloppy kisses doesn't make a relationship,' I snapped. 'So are you going to tell me why you've been slagging me off to the entire college?'

She had the grace to look embarrassed about that. 'Oh. Dylan and I have got unfinished business and there's all this stuff going on with Paul and Shona and me.'

'What are you talking about, Mia?'

She smiled nastily. 'Oh, Edie finally gets a clue! Everyone knows that Dylan and I had this really heavy thing going until Paul totally fell in love with me. Dylan was absolutely gutted but he understood that he had to let me go but Shona has this stupid crush on Paul. She, like, tries to throw herself at him and he's beyond mortified and just wants her off his back. So I told her you weren't really into Dylan, you were just using him to get close to Paul, so she'd come after you instead. Like, he walked you home once, didn't he?'

'YOU DID WHAT?' I screamed at her. I didn't even care that the whole canteen could hear.

'Clever wasn't it?'

I was overcome with a murderous rage. I yanked her out of the chair by her lapels. She stopped looking so smug.

'You evil cow,' I hissed at her. 'Thanks for ruining

my life.' I suddenly let go of her and she sank back into her seat.

'You're mad,' she sneered. 'As if Dylan'd fancy a kid like you. He just wanted to make me jealous. He told me that you'd be all right once puberty kicked in and . . .'

'Why don't you shut the hell up, Mia,' said Dylan from somewhere behind me.

I turned round to glare at him. He glared right back at me. In my head I see him in soft focus but when he's standing in front of me he's all hard lines and angles.

'I was only letting Edie know the gossip,' Mia laughed. 'She told me some interesting things about you too. Like, you're a "sloppy kisser" . . .'

I got out of there. Sharpish.

1st December

Everything makes sense now. How could I have been so stupid? I love Dylan. Dylan loves Mia. Mia loves Paul. So does Shona. But what really hurts is that Dylan's been stringing me along; using me to make Mia jealous. I just want to curl up and die. I can't bear to feel like this. I told Mum that I wasn't going back to college. I'd have to do A-levels with a home tutor or something. She was yelling at me and I was storming upstairs and yelling back when the doorbell rang. Mum answered it while I carried on shouting.

'It's for you, Edie,' Mum snapped. 'Stop acting like a three-year-old and come downstairs.'

Mothers must take special lessons in humiliating their offspring 'cause when I looked round Dylan was standing on the doorstep.

I felt all my blood rush down to my toes and I steadied myself on the banister.

'Tell him to come back when I've reached puberty,' I screeched in an incredibly mature fashion before running into my bedroom and slamming the door.

I was so busy crying that I didn't hear a gentle tapping on the door, but I did hear Dylan when he called: 'Edie! Are you all right? Can I come in?'

I wanted him to go. To turn around and go down the stairs and walk out of my life and never come back. I also really wanted to be able to stop crying. There's always such a lot of mucus involved.

'Come on, Edie. Are you going to let me in?' Dylan called softly again.

I was frozen to the spot, or rather, I pulled a pillow over my head. What was Mum thinking of? She wouldn't even let my five-year-old boy cousin into my room and now she'd invited Dylan up. I staggered up off the bed, where I'd collapsed, and half-heartedly checked my reflection in the mirror. I looked revolting like a big cosmetics company had been squirting shampoo in my eyes or something. What's more, I was in my pyjama bottoms and a holey jumper.

There was another gentle knock and with a deep sigh I opened the door an inch and peered through the crack at Dylan. He shifted awkwardly. Dylan was embarrassed. That had to be a first.

'What do you want?' I asked icily.

'Hey, don't be so snotty.' He gave me *that* look. The one where he arches his left eyebrow and smiles crookedly. He didn't exactly push his way in, but all of a sudden he was there in my room. Then he sat on the edge of my bed and it was like the weirdest thing. *Dylan was in my room! Sitting on my bed! In my room on my bed!*

I stayed standing. I couldn't look at him. It was just too freaky to have him sitting there. But Dylan obviously thought that my silence was because I was still mad at him (which was kinda half true).

'I never said that to Mia,' he said fiercely. 'Y'know the stuff about puberty. You're one of the coolest girls I know.'

I could feel myself going red. 'Whatever! Like I can believe a word that either of you say,' I snapped.

He tugged at my hand and pulled me towards him, so I was sort of sitting on the bed and sort of sitting on his lap. If my mum walked in, she was going to have a *fit*.

'OK, I'm going to be straight with you,' he said, trying to cup my chin so I'd look at him, though I pulled away. He gave up in the end. 'Mia and I got off with each other once and I am attracted to her on one

46

level, but on another level, a much bigger level, she's a complete 'mare.'

I thought I was going to burst into tears again and I guess Dylan thought I was going to too 'cause he put his arm round me. I rested my head on his shoulder for one millisecond. Then I stopped myself.

'What about me? Why do you keep kissing me? Why do you keep playing these games with me?'

Dylan's arm tightened around my waist. ''Cause I fancy you too,' he admitted with a wry twist of his mouth. 'You can fancy two people at the same time. But I need someone way tougher than you, Edie.'

'I am tough,' I protested.

Dylan shook his head. 'No you're not. And if we went out, I'd keep hurting you and you'd do that thing with your face that makes me feel all guilty.'

I frowned and he gently cuffed my cheek. 'There!' he said with a tiny smile. 'That's exactly what I'm talking about.'

We were both speaking English but we weren't talking the same language. He was telling me all the reasons why we shouldn't be together and I just wanted him to kiss me.

'We can be friends,' he was saying. 'Really good friends and I'll sort out this mess with Shona.'

'Maybe. Maybe not,' I muttered, trying to disentangle myself from his arms. If he didn't want to date me then he wasn't going to get to snuggle.

But Dylan gathered me up in this huge bear hug and *ruffled the top of my hair*! I could have spat nails . . .

Then Dylan being Dylan, he was gone.

2nd December

I was still trying to make sense of Dylan's visit when Shona came calling. There'd been a time when I thought we were going to become best friends or something but the way she just dropped me without even having the decency to tell me why still stung.

I found her sitting on the doorstep after I'd popped out for emergency rations of Maltesers. She was clutching a tub of Ben & Jerry's Cookie Dough and a mix CD she'd made.

'I guess you pretty much hate me,' she said with a wry twist of her mouth and all I could do was half shrug my shoulders.

When we got to my room, she curled up on my giant beanbag and dipped a spoon into the ice cream. 'I understand if you don't want to be mates again after the way I've treated you but you need to understand why I acted like such a stone-cold bitch,' she began.

And then she told me all about her and Paul and how they'd spent six months eyeing each other up at clubs and parties before Dylan introduced them and they immediately got together. And that she thought they were crazy in love ('I would just be dying to see him, just counting out the hours until we'd be together again') until Mia had come between them. I s'pose I realised that Shona felt the same way about Paul as I do about Dylan but, God, at least she actually got to date Paul.

And then she looked up at me with her huge manga eyes. 'Sorry?' she half-asked.

I nodded and it was awkward for, like, one second and then she started crying and I started crying and we both sat there sniffing and clinking spoons as we each tried to bogart the chocolate chips.

31st December

I haven't written for a while but I suppose New Year's Eve is as good a time as any.

I went to Brighton for a family Christmas and, quite frankly, even my annoying little cousins and Grandma moaning on about her rheumatism was better than being here.

It's been four weeks and already I can tell that this stupid, poxy 'friend' thing with Dylan is never going to work. He'll call and ask if I want to go to the flicks with Shona and him and I just about *melt*. It hurts too much to be with him and it hurts too much not to be with him. Sometimes life is just so cruel . . .

I thought him wanting to be friends was just an excuse for him to let me down gently and not have to bother with me any more, but it's been the opposite. We go out all the time with Shona and Simon and he reckons that friendly (that bloody word again) means an arm round my shoulder and kissing me hello and goodbye. It's even worse when he phones up. He'll be talking about his James Bond sculpture (don't even ask) and I'll drift off and imagine that he's saying, 'Edie, I just want to grab you and kiss you,' when he's really saying, 'Edie, I just want to be the next Picasso.' Anyway Simon's having a New Year party tonight and I guess that if I start psyching myself up a few hours beforehand, I might be able to face Dylan without begging him to ravish me.

1st January

Spent morning in bed recovering from party. It was ace and completely hideous in equal measure. I'd been looking forward to it because I'm sad enough to treasure every moment I get to share air space with Dylan. And I wore this really beautiful dress I'd got for Christmas from my auntie who lives in Amsterdam. It's black lace with a red slip to go under it. Mum said it was too old for me but I wore it with bright red tights and my black Chuck Taylors and she decided that 'dressed down' it was acceptable. Though 'you'd look much nicer if you wore a pair of heels.' Like, I'd take fashion advice from a woman who only does neutral colours.

Anyway, the party started off fine. It was wall-to-wall art students but then Dylan came over and started talking to me. He was wearing a black shirt with the word 'Trash' scrawled on it and we talked about Christmas. Well, he talked about Christmas, I was being frothy and amusing about the green triangles in a tin of Quality Street, which was actually a metaphor for how much I loved him. Not surprisingly, he didn't get it.

Then the whole night went downhill like a bus with faulty brakes. Paul and Mia showed up as an 'official' couple and Shona disappeared off the face of the earth. I found her half an hour later in one of the bedrooms in tears and in Dylan's arms. I stood there trying not to think evil thoughts. I know she was upset but did she have to have one hand on Dylan's leg and the other clutching his shoulder?

They looked up and saw me and I was like, 'Are you OK?' Then Shona ranted for what seemed like ages about how Mia was a skanky bitch and Paul was just seeing her to mess with Shona's mind. I was ummming and aaaahing in the right places but I sort of sensed they wanted me to leave them the hell alone.

I hung out with Nat and Trent and one of their mates, Josh. He was really good-looking in a ridiculous, boy-band kinda way. We shimmied around the living room a bit. When I was dancing, I almost forgot about Dylan and Shona, and Mia glaring at me from behind the punchbowl. Almost forgot but didn't quite succeed.

Then it was practically midnight. Someone let off a bunch of party poppers and the countdown started. Everyone was shouting and screaming like it had never been midnight before. I stood there letting the noise wash all over me when suddenly Dylan was standing in front of me, laughing.

'You're not a joiner, are you Edie, hon?' he teased, before pulling me into his arms to give me a New Year kiss. But somewhere between the pulling and the kissing, our eyes locked and when our lips hit, the kiss knocked me into the middle of last week. I could feel Dylan's heart pounding, as I managed to summon up enough willpower to push him away.

'I need some fresh air,' I gasped, not looking at Dylan as I staggered into the garden.

I didn't see him after that. Probably because I skulked in the kitchen with Josh and bored him stupid by bleating on about how doomed my love for Dylan was. Gay boys are such good listeners.

2nd January

Shona and I mooched round the sales. She was still seething about Mia and Paul, but she perked up when I told her about my New Year kiss. (I wasn't going to say anything, but it just popped out.)

'Hmmm, he gave me a kiss too but there were no tongues involved,' Shona said with a grin.

I was just working up to a really crushing retort

when we bumped into Josh, who works at The Magic Roundabout, this really cool second-hand clothes shop. He asked me if I wanted to go to the flicks with him tonight. I said OK, 'cause he's funny and a girl can never have too many friends.

2nd January (later)
Oh dear. I don't know how this happened. One minute I was thinking that Josh was gay and I could tell him stuff that I wouldn't normally tell a boy, the next minute, he's holding my hand and telling me that he's seen me around town and fancied me for ages!

Y'know how sometimes, you end up doing things that aren't actually a good idea, just 'cause you can't think of a reason not to do them? I snogged Josh and agreed to go on *another* date with him.

Dylan is the heir to my heart; the one boy I will never, ever get enough of, but I have to face facts, it's just not going to happen. And Josh is really good-looking. God, am I really that shallow? Besides, now that I've got a *boyfriend*, I'll be out of bounds as far as Dylan's concerned. Well that's the plan . . .

28th January
Having a boyfriend really cuts into your diary time. Especially when Josh wants to see me, like, every night.

I mean, I like Josh, he's very sweet and we have a laugh, but he's so *clingy* and he agrees with everything

I say. Even when I rant about how hanging is too good for Nicole Scherzinger and how they should make death by firing squad legal, he agrees with me. And Josh loves Nicole Scherzinger. Not a point in his favour.

He wants to have all these meaningful conversations and he's constantly asking me, 'What are you thinking about?' And, y'know, a lot of the time I'm just thinking about shoes or what I'm going to have for dinner or when I'm actually going to find time to do my History of Art notes.

It works better when we actually go and do something, like see a film or go bowling. Otherwise, we have to sit there and talk about our feelings or get off with each other. The kissing's nice but there's no sparkage. I miss the sparkage.

5th February
Is it weird of me not to have told any of my friends that me and Josh are going out? I haven't told the 'rents because, like, that would never happen. I think Nat and Trent must know because they're friends with him but I haven't told Shona or Dylan.

I'm pretty sure I was going to but I didn't and now the longer I leave it, the harder it is. Josh and I have been seeing each other for over a month (he got me an anniversary card!) and owning up would just mean having to go into this big, garbled explanation about why I didn't tell them sooner. There's this little voice in my head that tells me that I haven't told Shona or Dylan because I still have a stupid dream that Dylan will realise he can't live without me. And that if I admit to them that I'm seeing Josh, then I have to admit it to myself. But it's not like I'm in denial. Hey, I know that I'm going out with Josh. Josh and me are fine together.

So why haven't I told the others?

11th February
Dylan called me today. And he's like, 'Soooooo, Valentine's Day on Sunday . . .'

I snorted derisively, because it seemed like the right thing to do.

There was a pause. 'Shona and me are having an anti-Valentine's party. We're going to stick pins in Barbie and Ken and watch slasher movies. Only our single friends are invited, so I immediately thought of you,' he drawled.

'Ha ha.'

It would have been a perfect opportunity to tell him about Josh but I didn't. I'm such a coward.

12th February
Josh met me for lunch.

I was just getting stuck into my pizza and wishing that Josh would unsling his arm from round my shoulder because it was making hand-to-mouth co-ordination slightly tricky when I looked out of the window and saw Dylan walking past.

Please don't notice me, I prayed, but of course, he had to glance in the window at the precise moment that Josh was trying to place a slobbery kiss on my cheek. Dylan narrowed his eyes and shook his head before stomping off.

'I've got to go,' I told Josh, distractedly.

''Kay. Love you,' he said, gazing into my eyes.

'Um, yeah, me too,' I mumbled and dashed outside, but Dylan was gone.

I looked for him in the art block but then I bumped into Martyn and promptly forgot all about Dylan. It takes a lot to send all thoughts of Dylan flying out of my head but it's the coolest thing! Martyn is planning a trip to Paris next month for our Photography class. Paris! Without my parents! And it would be my birthday while we're away. Plus, it's educational. This is going to be killer.

13th February

The day from hell. The 'rents think I'm too young to go to Paris on a supervised college trip with a bunch of 'feckless art students'. Jeez, I'm going to be seventeen next month. We had a big argument about it. Cue much door slamming and flouncing out of rooms. That was just my mum. I, of course, was the epitome of restraint. We were just in the middle of part four of the row when Dylan rang and asked me to lunch.

Now normally if Dylan asked me to meet him for lunch I'd be really excited but as I caught the bus into town I had this sick feeling of dread, like I was going to the dentist to have all my teeth filled without an anaesthetic.

I met Dylan outside Rhythm Records (where he works part-time) and he barely said hello. In fact, what came out of his mouth was definitely more of a grunt than any recognisable word.

We walked to the Arts Centre café in silence and it wasn't one of those companionable silences that we're normally so good at. It was spiky.

'So, what's up?' I asked after Dylan had sat and played with his pasta for fifteen minutes.

'Nothing.' Dylan was never usually that snippy with me.

'OK,' I said very warily because I had a feeling we were about to get into an argument and I really didn't want to go there.

Dylan looked up from his pasta and pesto and flared his nostrils. 'How's Josh?' Too late, looked like I was going to get one.

Then it was my turn to stare at my penne pollo e funghi like it was about to impart the secrets of the universe. 'I was going to tell you but, um, there was never a good moment,' I muttered.

Dylan pushed his plate away. 'How long's it been going on?'

'About six weeks. Not that it's any of your business.' I'd changed my mind about having an argument. He didn't want me so he didn't have the right to get all narked just because someone else did.

'He looks like he failed the auditions for One Direction,' Dylan suddenly spat out. 'I thought you had better taste.'

'Just 'cause he . . .' I was going to say something bitchy about Dylan but I thought better of it. This was Dylan and . . . *it was Dylan* and I couldn't bear for him to be angry with me.

I reached across the table and touched his hand. He didn't touch me back but he didn't pull away either.

'Oh D, I'm sorry I didn't tell you about Josh, but please let's not fall out. Please.'

For a second, I thought he was going to get hissy at me again but he turned my hand over and stroked the back of my knuckles.

'You're right,' Dylan said smoothly. 'But I still think he's a loser.'

I pulled a face at him. 'Whatever. Anyway have you heard about this Paris trip?'

'Yeah, I'm not going.'

'Why not? It'll be fun. Educational fun, what's not to like?' We were still holding hands. I don't even know if Dylan realised that he was still stroking the backs of my fingers.

'Can't afford it,' he said shortly, dropping my hand and picking up his fork. Dylan never talked about his family and stuff but Shona had told me that Dylan had to pay his own way.

I decided to change the subject. 'So am I allowed to come to your anti-Valentine's party or what?'

14th February

It sucks when Valentine's Day is on a Sunday and there's no post. But there were two cards waiting for me when I finally emerged from my bed.

One of them was from Josh. How did I know? He'd signed his name, that's how, and the soft focus, dew-dripping rose was just soooo Josh.

He'd also got me one of those hideous teddy bears that have 'I love you' written on their stomachs.

The other card was home-made and unsigned and featured a cartoon of me as a superhero complete with lightning flashes, and underneath the words 'She's Electric'.

It could only be from Dylan, couldn't it?

26th February

I got woken up at the crack of dawn by the doorbell.

Mum had already gone to work so I had to stagger out of bed and stomp down the stairs, swearing each step of the way, to find Shona leaning on the bell.

'Sorry, did I wake you up?' asked Shona, not sounding at all repentant. 'It's so cool, they've opened up places on the French trip to the entire college and I'm going!'

'Great,' I mumbled, though it *was* great, especially as I'd worn the 'rents down through the medium of nagging and my place was guaranteed, deposit paid. 'Now go away. I'm having a lie-in.'

'There's no time for that,' Shona snorted. 'We have to plan what we're going to wear!'

Before I kicked her out, I promised to meet up with her in the college canteen later.

When I managed to make it into college a couple of hours later, Dylan was hanging out with Shona. As I walked towards them, he looked me up and down. It made me feel all hot and bothered in a way that Josh's kisses never did. Getting to their table seemed to take forever and I was painfully aware of every bit of me. Of how lanky my limbs were and the spot on my top where I'd tried to cover up some nail varnish spillage by sewing a tiny flower patch on it.

When I pulled out a chair, Dylan raised his eyebrows at me like I'd asked him a question and he wanted me to repeat it but I just screwed up my face in a fair approximation of a smile and tried not to look at him. Some days it's like that – he's just too much.

Shona couldn't stop talking about Paris. I think she's desperate for anything that will take her mind off the fact that Paul and Mia are still an item. But Dylan was like, 'Can't you shut up about the bloody French trip? It's getting so boring.'

Then he asked me if I'd been on any good dates lately, and when I blushed and began stammering about ten-pin bowling, he started laughing. Sometimes I really hate Dylan.

7th March

Latest news on the Paris trip is that Mia's going. Shona is practically vibrating about it. I swear to God, I thought she was going to literally levitate when she told me. And I had Josh on the phone first thing this morning asking if he could come. *And he doesn't even go to our college.* I was trying really hard to be supportive of Shona but by lunchtime she was doing my head in, so I pretended I had to run some 'rent-type errands. I was sitting in the park, chucking bits of the chicken sandwich I'd abandoned at the ducks, when I saw Dylan on the other side of the pond. I didn't think he'd seen me but he waved.

'Meet you halfway,' he shouted. The irony of his words was not lost on me.

It was very romantic. We sat on a bench under the weeping willow, hidden from the rest of the world. Dylan was, God, just being utterly adorable. I'd forgotten what it was like to be on the receiving end of his sultry looks. He *has* to practise them in front of the mirror. There can be no other explanation. This little half-smile plays along his lips, his eyes glint and his voice drops to a conspiratorial whisper. It makes me feel all unnecessary.

When I asked him if he minded not going to Paris Dylan just shrugged and said Paris was just like Manchester but with French people. And I was like, 'Yeah and the Eiffel Tower,' and even though it was the feeblest joke in the world, he laughed.

9th March

Weird! I bumped into Dylan ambling down my road, even though he lives on the other side of town. For one moment my heart leapt at the thought that he'd come to see me and to hell with having to go forty-five minutes out of his way. That little illusion lasted the five seconds it took Dylan to say: 'What are you doing here?'

I huffed indignantly, 'I live here, remember.'

Dylan was acting very strangely (even for him). In fact, he was being positively shifty, shuffling his feet, tugging at his Trash shirt and refusing to look at me. I was just about to walk off when he suddenly blurted out that he was painting a portrait of this woman's cat to get some extra money and did I want to go with him?

Turns out the woman was Mrs Williams across the road. Her cat, Henry, is fat and mean and not a quarter as nice as Pudding. I had to hold the spiteful little bastard still while Dylan made sketches. I nearly got scratched to death, but it was almost worth it to see Dylan being well-behaved. When Mrs Williams asked if we 'were courting', he joked that she was the only woman in his life. He's such a flirt. I liked watching him work though. He was completely focussed on the sketches, staring intently at me and the furiously wriggling Henry and then glancing down at his pad. When Dylan concentrates his forehead scrunches up and the tip of his tongue pokes out of the corner of his mouth. It's very guh-making.

It would have been easy to fool myself that all that attention was for me and only for me. But it wasn't. It was for a bad-tempered, overweight ginger cat. Ho hum.

It was dark when we finally left. Mrs Williams had force fed us so much home-made Madeira cake (which, actually, yum) that I felt kinda queasy. I was wondering what I should do; whether I should invite Dylan back for tea 'cause it was late. But then he'd have to sit down in front of the suspicious and over-protective gaze of my father, who had once said (in a not very jokey way) that he didn't plan on letting me date until I was at least thirty.

I was deep in thought about how to prolong this

unexpected Dylan contact without having to formally introduce him to either of my primary care givers when he suddenly flinched. 'I've got an eyelash in my eye,' he groaned.

He pulled me under a lamp-post and squinted down at me. 'Can you see it?'

Then we had to do the whole 'pull your eyelid down, look up, look down, look at the tree' thing until I said, 'Yeah, hold still,' and 'cause it was an emergency, I licked the corner of a tissue and tried to gently ease the lash out. It worked first time and then I realised how close we were standing. I think Dylan did too 'cause he lowered his head like he was about to kiss me. Our lips were nearly touching – all I had to do was move my mouth a couple of millimetres and we'd be kissing.

'I'll see you tomorrow,' he drawled, kissing me on the forehead like I was five and loping off.

Aaaaaaaaargh!

10th March

I realised while I was walking to college that the extra money Dylan was getting for painting Henry could pay for the Paris trip. But when I asked him, he practically bit my head off. In fact, he said that he *would* bite my head off and flush it down the nearest toilet if I mentioned the words 'French' and 'trip' ever again in his hearing.

'He's acting weird,' I moaned at Shona.

'He *is* weird,' she replied sagely.

I decided to avoid Dylan for the rest of the day but when I came out of my English class he was lurking in the corridor.

'So, d'you reckon I need to pack my nicest hoodie?' he asked me, following me to my locker.

'What are you going on about?' I said in my most withering voice.

'I'm asking for some sartorial advice on what to wear in Paris, of course,' he said sarcastically. 'Oh yeah, I forgot to tell you that I'm going, didn't I?'

I glared at him. 'I really hate you!'

'Sure you do, Edie,' Dylan purred. 'Anyway have to go. Shopping to do and stuff.'

I was going to kill him before we got to Paris. Fact.

But, big squeeeeeee!, Dylan's coming to Paris with me (and forty-eight other people). Yay!

15th March

This time on Saturday I'll be on my way to *la ville de Paris*. That is, if my mother actually lets me leave the house. She's stressing-out in a major way. It's not like it's the first time that I've been away without her and Dad to remind me to do my coat up or check if I've got credit on my phone. I was like, 'You weren't this bad when I went to Brownie camp.'

'But I can't believe I'll miss your birthday,' she said, her voice going all squeaky.

'Well, you can give me my present to take with me,' was not the right thing for me to say, as I realised as soon as the words had left my mouth and her face kinda collapsed in on itself.

She wanted me to tell her that I was going to miss her and how my birthday wouldn't be the same without her and Dad having an argument about whether I was too old to still have candles on my cake. But it would have given her too much satisfaction. Then she tried to play with my hair. I reckon she's having a mid-life crisis or something.

Anyway, I've got more important things to worry about. Like, how will I cope spending five days in close proximity with Dylan? And will he try to kiss me again? And will I manage to be strong and stick to my decision to make a go of this thing with Josh? Josh is nice, super-nice, in fact, but I'm not sure if I want nice. All I know is that when I see Dylan and he gives me *that* look (the one where I get the feeling he can see through my clothes or something) I could forget that Josh ever existed.

All this stuff rocketing round my head just makes me want to eat copious amounts of chocolate.

16th March

Shona's invited herself over to stay tomorrow night. The official reason is so Dad can give us a lift to the coach on Friday but really she's coming round so she can cut my fringe, make a couple of playlists and help me plan my Paris capsule wardrobe.

The trip has become all about the clothes. We were sitting in the canteen just before I went off to Photography and all we could talk about was what we were going to wear.

'Y'know how all those famous people reckon that they have one black dress, one pair of jeans, a cardie and two simple T-shirts that they can dress up or dress down?' I whined. 'Well, I don't get it. How do I know what I'll feel like wearing on Monday? Or what hairslides will suit my mood on Wednesday morning?'

'It's all rubbish, Edie,' snorted Shona. 'Famous people have walk-in closets stuffed full of designer outfits. And they get free clothes to go to swank parties in.'

'It sucks,' I said with such vehemence that Shona looked at me in surprise. 'And they have stylists to help them put together their outfits.'

'Even Ke$ha,' Shona said, holding up her copy of *Heat*, which showed a picture of Ke$ha wearing something that looked like an explosion in a denim factory. 'But you've got something that Ke$ha hasn't. You have fashion sense.'

She was right, I did. 'And every morning I wake up and thank God for my unique ability to accessorise!'

I giggled and even Shona managed to crack a smile,

which was all that she'd allow herself when she thought something was really funny. Then suddenly I was plunged into darkness as someone put their hands over my eyes and a deep voice said, 'Guess who?'

I knew it was Dylan. I could smell the old leather of his jacket and the faint scent of oil-based paints. I didn't know what to do. If I told him that I knew it was him, then it'd look as if I was really sad and obsessed. And if I just ignored him, I'd look stupid and like I couldn't take a joke. So I just sat there frozen, kind of revelling in the touch of his hands on my face.

'I think it's an Art Boy,' I said at last. 'Yup, I can definitely smell Art Boy.'

He took his hands away, brushing my cheek as he did so.

'Edie's having trouble planning her outfits for Paris,' said Shona with another smile. That was almost two in five minutes, she was going to have to watch that.

Dylan gave me a knowing look. 'What? You can't decide which Marc Jacobs dress to pack?' he asked me with a teasing smile.

I stuck my tongue out at him and then wondered if that was the wrong signal to send out to someone who was just a friend. 'It's OK for you. All you have to decide is which pair of tatty jeans and faded T-shirt to wear.'

He failed to rise to the bait. 'They may seem like tatty jeans and faded T-shirts to the untrained eye,'

Dylan informed me smugly, 'but they're actually really expensive designer clothes that just look like I found them in a skip.'

'That job in Rhythm Records must pay really well,' muttered Shona archly.

Dylan ran a hand through his hair, mussing it up and I itched to smooth it down. 'I've just spent the last week doing a portrait of this woman's cat to get some extra cash. It was a nightmare. Look.'

He pulled up the sleeve of his jacket to show two long cat scratches on the underside of his forearm. I couldn't stop myself. I reached out a finger and touched the raised wound on the soft skin.

'Nasty,' I mumbled. I hadn't realised that Shona was clueless about the pet portrait. I thought Dylan told her everything. I guess, he was worried that his couldn't-give-a-fuck image would be shot to pieces if word got out that he was drawing old women's pets to make a bit of cash for the trip to Paris.

'You coming to class, Eeds?' Dylan called over his shoulder as he'd already started walking away.

'I'll see you later,' I said to Shona, picking up my bag and walking over to Dylan who was waiting impatiently by the canteen doors.

But I wished that I had skived off Photography because Dylan was being so *scratchy*.

'You seeing the devoted Josh before you leave?' he

whispered to me, as Martyn banged on about our itinerary for Paris.

'I'm seeing him tonight, if you must know,' I hissed crossly. 'Not that it's any business of yours.'

'I bet he'll hold your hand and get all mopey 'cause you're going to be away for five whole days. How will he manage without you?'

'Very well, I should imagine,' I snapped.

'Yeah, right! He needs help crossing the road.'

I shot him an extra special version of no. 3 from my evil glare collection.

'Temper, temper,' laughed Dylan, reaching out and grabbing my wrist. I tried to pull my hand away.

'What are you doing?'

'I'm just checking your pulse. Stress isn't very good for you,' Dylan said with a smirk.

'Well, stop bugging me then.'

Dylan was right. Josh took me to Pizza Express and spent an hour going on about how much he was going to miss me and how great I was and how he wouldn't know what to do with himself.

It's flattering going out with a boy who thinks you're completely ace, but sometimes I don't know who this girl is that Josh thinks he's so in love with. It doesn't sound like me.

'You won't know I'm gone,' I insisted. 'Five days is, like, no time at all.'

Josh pushed his floppy blond fringe out of his eyes and I wanted to scream at him to get his hair cut.

'But I really wanted us to spend your birthday together,' he moaned.

I picked at a cold piece of garlic bread. 'Look, Josh, I wish you were coming too, but you're not so we'll just have to make the best of it.'

Josh just sighed heavily, which made me grit my teeth with irritation, and asked if I was going to finish the garlic bread.

Josh walked me home and stopped when he got to the corner of my road.

'What's up?' I asked, hoping we weren't going to have yet another discussion about me going to Paris.

'Since I'm not going to see you on your birthday, I thought I'd give you your present now,' he said, his voice trembling a little.

I thought that this was his cue to grab me and kiss my face off – Dylan would – but instead he was rummaging in his pocket. Eventually, along with a couple of bus tickets and some bits of fluff, he produced a small, wrapped present.

'You can open it now if you like,' he said but I was already tearing off the paper to uncover a jewellery box.

For one terrifying moment I thought it was an

engagement ring and he was going to do something really stupid like propose to me. As I opened the box, I was rehearsing how I'd tell him that I was too young to commit myself, but it wasn't a ring, it was a gold necklace with a charm that said 'I love you' on it. I don't want to sound like an ungrateful bitch, but it was dead naff. Josh looked at me expectantly and I couldn't hurt his feelings. I reached up and gave him a kiss on the cheek. 'Thanks Josh. It's lovely,' I lied. And then before he could reach for me, I gave his hand a quick squeeze, muttered something about my curfew and ran the last few yards home.

17th March
Shona was very underwhelmed when she saw the token of Josh's affection.

'Not really you, Edie,' she said, wrinkling her nose when I showed her the necklace.

'It was probably really expensive but I don't like gold,' I muttered, trying not to sound like a heartless ingrate. 'I'd much rather have had, y'know, maybe one of those red enamel strawberries on a silver chain that we saw in town last week.'

'Hmmm, that sounds far more like something Dylan would get a girl,' Shona mused with an arch look in my direction.

'Oh, shut up!'

'Come on Edie, I know you're still mad about him,'

Shona insisted. 'All this "being friends" stuff doesn't fool me. And when we get to romantic Paris, the city of lovers, who knows what might happen?'

I threw a balled-up pair of socks at her. 'Yeah, Shona, who knows what might happen? Like, you could knock off Mia and get back with Paul.'

Shona raised her eyebrows, 'Something like that, perhaps.'

I sat down next to her on the bed. 'Spill.'

She stopped folding cardies and gave me a long look. 'I *am* going to get back with Paul,' she said fiercely. 'Not *if*, but *when*. Mia's just a temporary blip. I bet you a tenner that by the time we get back from Paris, Paul will be glued to my side.'

I shrugged. 'You sound like you've got it all worked out.'

'You bet.' Shona dug into her bag and squashed everything down to make more room. 'I will end her if I have to.'

She sounded positively scary and then I saw the box of condoms she was packing. I guess that if I thought about it, Shona and Paul probably had slept with each other (or at least thought about it) but there was no way that I was ready to get naked and horizontal with Dylan or Josh. Or, like, anyone for that matter.

'Oh! So you and Paul were . . . y'know, sort of doing it?'

'Well, yeah,' she laughed. 'We're both nineteen. I forget what a baby you are.'

'I'll be seventeen next week,' I pointed out.

'So, you're sweet sixteen now and never been kissed! Well, Dylan had something different to say on *that* particular subject.'

I glared at her, but she was lying back on the bed, giggling at her own wit.

'Are we going to do this packing or what?'

Shona and I realised that if we combined our wardrobes, we'd both have twice as many outfits to go away with, but it was impossible to narrow down our fashion selections any further.

'Do you really think we need to change for dinner every night?' I asked doubtfully.

''Course. We need daywear for all that mooching around art galleries and evening wear for dining and clubbing.'

'But jeans and leggings and jumpers are daywear, Shona, not cocktail dresses,' I protested. All she'd packed was my entire collection of vintage frocks and beaded cardies. In her suitcase.

'Huh! I laugh in the face of daywear,' said Shona grandly.

I started taking some of my stuff out of her suitcase. 'I know we agreed to share our clothes but I seem to be the only one giving here.'

Shona was idly flicking through my old CDs. She turned round to look at me, her eyes narrowing slightly.

'What?' I asked defensively, wondering if she'd found the McFly album that I'd hidden.

'I was just thinking about how much you've changed since I first met you,' Shona said. 'You used to be really quiet, you wouldn't say boo to a goose. And now you're very mouthy. But in a good way,' she added hastily when I shot her a look.

'It was really hard moving to a new town,' I muttered, sitting down on the bed again. I was suffering from severe packing fatigue. 'When I started at college, Mia was the only person who talked to me, then she turned out to be a complete psycho. I felt like I had nobody to talk to, that everyone hated me. And I was really in awe of you, and Dylan, and Paul and Simon.'

Shona sat down next to me and chuckled. 'God, we thought you hated us. You always seemed to be in your own world. Sometimes I'd catch you looking at me like, like I'd just crawled out of the nearest rubbish dump.'

'No I didn't! I guess I've just got one of those faces. Besides, Mia told me that you and Dylan had some weird relationship where you'd get off with loads of people to make each other jealous.'

'Mia!' Shona said disparagingly. 'How does she think of these things? Look, Dylan and I have known each other since nursery school. Snogging him would be like sucking face with my brother.'

'Ewwwww.'

'Exactly!'

The packing took forever. I was so intent on organising the right combination of clothes and ripping tunes onto my iPod to listen to on the coach that it was two in the morning before I finally finished. Shona was already taking up most of the bed. She raised herself up on one elbow to survey my stuffed suitcase.

'I can't get the stupid thing to shut,' I snarled, trying to force the top down.

'Edie, this might be a really stupid question, but have you actually remembered to pack your camera?'

Doh! 'I knew there was something I'd forgotten.'

Shona rolled her eyes. 'And the fact that it's primarily a trip for your Photography class just flew out of your head, right?'

'You got any room in your suitcase?'

It took another half hour to take everything out and start again. By the time I got into bed, Shona was fast asleep. I pushed her over to her side and re-claimed half of the duvet that she was hogging and tried to get myself into a sleepy frame of mind, but my head was buzzing.

'Shona, you awake?'

'No. What is it?'

'Do you think Dylan fancies me?'

'Um . . .'

'I mean, has he said anything to you?'

'Go to sleep, Edie.'

Diary Two, Paris

I know I'm going to get a severe dosage of repetitive strain injury but I have to write down everything that happened in Paris now that I'm finally back. Everything. Not how things tasted and looked and felt; all that travelogue malarkey. But the important stuff. What was said and done and every nuance and inflection of the saying and the doing. Just so I have proof that I was there and it wasn't a dream. Although I guess at times it seemed more like a nightmare. And now everything's different; things can't go back. It's like I'm not the same person any more, I've changed in all sorts of huge, important ways. But if you looked at me, you wouldn't necessarily be able to tell.

Plus there was serious shopping. So I'm going to write it all down now. In one go. And I'm not going to skip bits.

Friday
So it started like this.

One minute I was looking at the clock and it was four in the morning, the next I could hear my mother yelling at me to get up.

'Go 'way,' I groaned, burrowing further into the pillows.

'Edith! I won't tell you again. It's seven o'clock; you have to leave in half an hour. Shona's already up and dressed.'

I opened one eye. Mum and Shona were standing over me.

I showed willing and inched one leg out from under the duvet.

Mum sighed. 'I haven't got time for this. Shona, see if you can get her up, love. I'll go and finish making breakfast.'

Shona obviously didn't believe in Mum's gentle approach to getting me up, which is why I was shocked into full consciousness by what felt like a bucket of cold water being thrown over me.

'You bitch!'

Shona physically hauled me out of bed. 'I didn't know your name was Edith,' she grinned.

'And nobody else had better find out,' I hissed, staggering to the bathroom.

'You're not a morning person are you, kid?'

I just had time to give her the finger before I slammed the bathroom door.

We were the last ones to get on the coach. We'd held everyone up for fifteen minutes and clambered on to a round of sarcastic applause.

Martyn and his hippy girlfriend, Tania (who'd come along to help), started telling us off in a very unhippy-like manner.

'It's Edie's fault,' protested Shona while I glared at her out of the piggy slits that used to be my eyes. 'She wouldn't get out of bed.'

'Really, Eddie . . .' began Tania, her braless breasts swinging agitatedly.

'It's Edie!' Shona and I said in unison.

I could see Dylan signalling to us from halfway down the coach. There was a double seat in front of him and Simon; an empty seat just waiting for me so I could talk to Dylan in the gap between the headrests. I staggered down the aisle after Shona, while Tania followed us, still going on and on about my time-keeping. I could tell that she was going to be a major pain in the butt.

I tried to get my shoulder bag in the overhead locker, but I was so stupid with sleep that I couldn't manage it.

Dylan rose from his seat. 'Let me do it for you.'

He was wearing a new pair of dark jeans (I'm sad enough to have his whole wardrobe committed to memory), a Beatles T-shirt and his scruffy leather jacket. As he reached up to put my bag away, his T-shirt rose up and I half-shut my eyes rather than look at his stomach, but I still got a glimpse. It wasn't a six-pack, but it was sort of taut. Then I realised that he might have seen my tummy when I was trying to put my bag away. It might have been lack of sleep, it might have been the boiled egg that Mum had forced me to eat before we left (one of the reasons why we were so late), but seeing Dylan's stomach and wondering if he'd seen mine made me feel slightly sick.

I grunted something at him that might have been thank you and slumped down next to Shona.

She was busy telling Simon and Dylan exactly why we were so late.

'Well, then Edie discovered that she'd packed the jeans and jumper that she was meant to be wearing today, then she had a fight with her mum about eating a proper breakfast and then we were just about to leave when she realised that she hadn't bought any film for her camera so we had to stop at a newsagent's on the way. We had to go to three of them before we found one that sold black-and-white film.'

'Remind me not to ask you for a character reference if I'm ever up in court,' I snapped.

Shona pulled a face at Simon and Dylan. 'She's been like this ever since she got up.'

'You're obviously not a morning person, Edie,' said Dylan. 'I'll have to remember that.'

'That's exactly what I said to her and she did something very rude with one of her fingers,' teased Shona.

Silence was definitely the best form of defence. I peered round the coach. Mia and Paul, looking all snuggly-wuggly, were sitting at the back near Nat and Trent who waved at me. I summoned up enough energy to raise a hand in their direction.

It was going to be hours before we got to Dover. I snuggled down into the folds of my dark green jumper and shut my eyes. It was funny, the night before, I couldn't sleep at all because I was thinking about Dylan, but that morning, when he was just inches away from me, I couldn't stop myself from nodding off.

We'd been on the coach for five hours and every time I went to sleep, we stopped at yet another motorway service station. And I couldn't be left sleeping on the coach, oh no. According to Tania, I could be attacked by a homicidal, axe-wielding maniac, so Shona had to wake me up and drag me across the car park. To make matters worse, she got Dylan to do it once. I could feel someone's hands shaking me gently and I'm ashamed to say he got one of my fists in his face (I'm not a good riser, OK?).

When a Dylan-like voice said, 'Ow,' I quickly opened my eyes to see him crouched in front of me, rubbing his cheek.

'Sorry,' I mumbled.

'I hope you don't do that to Josh when he tries to wake you up,' Dylan drawled.

I gasped. 'He's never been with me when I'm asleep. I mean, I haven't . . . We're not . . . It's none of your business!'

I pushed past him and practically ran down the aisle and off the coach.

The next time I fell asleep, I knew I had a clear two hours before we stopped at Dover. I was just settling into a really good dream about, well, never mind, when I was startled awake by some icy-cold liquid drenching me for the second time that day.

'What the . . . ?!'

'Ooops, sorry Edie.' Mia was standing over me with an upended can of Diet Coke. 'We must have hit a pothole.'

'Yeah, right,' spat Shona, who'd also got doused. 'There's loads of potholes on motorways.'

Mia shrugged. 'Whatever. I hope it doesn't stain.'

'I'm soaked,' I whimpered. I could feel the Coke seeping into the seat underneath me. My jeans were wet through.

'Oh Edie, you look like you've been caught short,' Mia giggled.

'Do me a favour, Mia – go and play in the traffic.'

'Some people are *so* touchy,' she smirked before sauntering back to Paul.

'I think I put a pair of leggings in my shoulder bag,' said Shona helpfully. 'Like, if you want to change.'

I shook my head. 'I can't take off my jeans in front of everyone.'

'I guess not.'

This trip was turning into a nightmare. I'd humiliated myself at least three times in front of Dylan. Mia was obviously planning on being a complete bitch on wheels for the next five days and it looked like I'd wet myself.

'D'you want some chocolate?' said Shona, shoving an Aero at me. 'It might cheer you up.'

I turned it down. Not even an Aero could help me right then.

Fortunately the ferry crossing helped me get my own back on the world. The Channel was choppy and practically everyone on the boat was puking up. The scene in the ladies' toilet was like this painting I'd once seen called *Descent into the Inferno*. People were even hurling into the washbasins. Luckily, I have a cast-iron constitution. It takes more than a little rough sea to make me sick. In fact, it was really peaceful sitting on the deck, feeling the salt-water spray sting my face. It was one of those times when you know that you're really alive. You're aware of all of your senses. I could hear the sea whooshing against the sides of the boat, I could smell and taste the tang of the air and even though the water was a murky blue, the white-tipped waves running along the top of it looked like little frills of lace. I sat there, feeling at one with the elements until I got a bit bored, so I dug out my phone and sat there like a dweeby boy with my hood up. I'd just got to level eight on Tetris when Dylan sat down beside me.

'I thought you'd be puking somewhere,' I said, concentrating on slotting shapes into place.

'Nah, I've got a stomach like an ox,' Dylan explained, leaning forward and resting his elbows on his knees.

'Hmmm, me too. Oh, hell,' I added as I screwed up the next level of the game. 'Look, I'm sorry about before, about hitting you, I mean. I'm a bit disorientated when I first wake up.'

'Don't worry about it,' said Dylan lightly. 'You're not the first girl to hit me, you won't be the last.'

'Who hit you?' I asked.

'Mia hit me once when we were sort of seeing each other,' he muttered.

My chest felt like it had just caved in.

'You never said you went out with her, you just said that you'd got off with her,' I blurted out, before I could stop myself.

Dylan turned and looked at me. 'We didn't go out on dates, we'd just go round to each other's houses and fool about.'

For starters, I've never been round to Dylan's house. Secondly, all those times that he'd kissed me, was that just 'fooling about'? Thirdly, why did I give him every opportunity to say things that I knew I didn't want to hear and fourthly . . .

'You've gone again,' Dylan remarked.

'What?'

'You do it all the time, Edie. I'll be talking to you and you just disappear somewhere inside of yourself,' he whispered, leaning back on the seat so his head was close to mine. 'Anyway what are you doing, sitting here by yourself?'

I started to tell him about the stuff I'd been thinking before, about how alive I felt with the sea roaring underneath me. Dylan was staring at me intently while I spoke. Then he did the most curious thing. He reached out one of his long-fingered hands and pulled down my hood.

Immediately, the wind tugged at my hair, blowing it in every direction. Dylan caught a bunch of it and pulled it gently. 'Your hair's amazing. It's the colour of clear honey.'

Our faces were so close by now, I could see that his eyes weren't completely green; there were flecks of brown around the pupils. God, he had the longest boy-lashes.

I felt like I was caught up in the middle of someone else's dream as I touched his hair, which was ruffling in the wind too.

'Your hair's the colour of . . . really dark chocolate,'

I said. 'It looks black but when you get nearer, it's a rich, dark brown.' I smiled and he rubbed a finger across my mouth.

We stayed like that for at least five minutes, honestly. Sitting so close together that our knees bumped against each other. And Dylan ran his fingers over my face. Across my eyelids and my eyebrows. Down my cheeks. Along my chin. But mostly he touched my mouth, running his fingers over my lips again and again until they were tingling.

But he didn't kiss me. And it didn't matter that he didn't kiss me because although his kisses sucked the soul right out of me, the feel of his hands on my face felt even better in a strange kind of way. Like, in my whole life I'll probably kiss lots of people and most of those kisses I'll probably forget, but I know I'll always remember those minutes on the ferry to France when I sat with Dylan and he stroked my face as if it was the most precious thing in his world.

It couldn't last forever. But it lasted until Simon appeared and promptly threw up over the railings.

'I knew I shouldn't have had that beer,' he groaned when he finally came up for air.

It made me start giggling, I don't know why. Poor Simon was green-faced. But once I started giggling, I couldn't stop. It quickly upgraded itself to a full-on belly laugh, which started Dylan off too. Simon looked at us in disgust, like we were a pair of complete retards, while we laughed so hard that tears ran down our faces.

'I'm going to find Shona,' said Simon huffily.

When we got back on the coach, Simon and Shona were slumped against each other, fast asleep, so I had no choice but to sit next to Dylan. No choice at all.

I scooched around so my back was against the window and my legs were pulled up against my body, but when Dylan sat down he patted his thighs and I propped my legs over them. He rested one of his hands on my knee, but not in a lecherous, copping-a-feel kinda way.

'Are you sleepy?' he asked.

'Are you kidding?' I snorted. 'I spent most of the morning asleep. Are you?'

'Nah, I never sleep much.' He gave me a look from under his lashes that didn't seem entirely innocent. 'Well, how are we going to pass the time?'

I looked round the coach. The lights were dimmed and most people were asleep; it was only mid-afternoon but I guess all that puking had taken it out of them. Sitting there with my legs draped across Dylan suddenly felt very intimate.

'We could play the alphabet game,' I said, trying to lighten the atmosphere.

'What's that?'

'We list things we'd take to a, erm, I don't know, a festival, but we have to do it alphabetically and you have to list all the things that we've said before, otherwise you lose.'

Dylan smirked. 'So what happens when you lose? Do you have to pay a forfeit?'

I gave him a look. It was a pretty good look – most people wouldn't have wanted to be on the other end of it. 'Nothing like that, young man.'

Dylan raised one of his eyebrows. 'I don't know what you think I was thinking. OK, if I lose, I'll buy you a week's supply of chocolate.'

'And if I lose?'

'Oh, I'm sure I'll think of something.'

'. . . So, I went to the festival and I took articles of clothing belonging to Louis Walsh, Brillo pads, chocolate cake, damp-proofing, an egg casserole and a full-scale, working model of a sewage station,' Dylan chanted.

'I went to the festival and I took articles of clothing belonging to Louis Walsh, brine shrimp, a chemistry textbook, damp-proofing, an egg casserole, a full-scale, working model of a sewage station and a erm, Greek salad.'

'Time out,' called Dylan suddenly. 'How come all the stuff you're taking to this hypothetical festival is food?'

Ha! I was so going to win! Talk about a transparent stalling manoeuvre. 'Firstly, there's nothing in the rules about what kind of stuff I can take to the festival and secondly, if you don't have your go in the next ten seconds, you're out.'

'All right, but I think we should play a different game now,' Dylan announced with a glint in his eye.

I stiffened suspiciously. 'What kind of game?'

'Who would you rather?'

'No way!' I spluttered.

'Oh, come on, I'll start. Who would you rather, the ugliest one out of One Direction or Brooklyn Beckham?'

I rolled my eyes. 'God, Dylan, how young do you think I am? Aren't they both, like, twelve?'

'You've got to choose,' Dylan insisted, curling his tongue up between his front teeth in a way which made my insides *ache*.

'OK, One Direction boy, I guess. At least he's probably past the age of consent,' I finally decided. 'Who would you rather, Cheryl Cole or the posh one out of the Saturdays?'

'Cheryl, definitely,' said Dylan instantly. 'She's going through stuff and I'd like to help her out with that.'

'Whatever, Mr Perv. Why are you smiling like that?'

Dylan was grinning in a cat that got the cream kind of way. 'Oh, I've just thought of a really good one for you. Who would you rather, Josh or . . . me?'

I could feel myself going bright red. 'That's not fair!' It was a whole world of not fair, to be more accurate.

'Just answer the question, missy,' Dylan drawled.

'If I answer that, then you have to tell me who you'd rather, me or Mia?'

It was Dylan's turn to look uncomfortable. 'OK, you've made your point, I guess. Let's pretend I never asked you that question.'

'So you'd rather kiss Mia?' I couldn't believe that we'd got into this don't-go-there topic of conversation. And I couldn't believe that my voice was saying things even when I was telling it to shut up.

'I never said that!' protested Dylan.

I tried to shift my legs off him, but he suddenly grabbed hold of one of my calves.

'Let go of my leg,' I hissed.

'No! Just calm down,' he whispered fiercely.

'I am sodding calm,' I practically screamed at him. 'Just tell me who was a better kisser, me or Mia?'

'Well, I'm not snogging Mia, am I?' Dylan said cryptically.

'You're not snogging me either,' I reminded him with a slight wobble to my voice.

'I could if I wanted to,' Dylan bit out. 'But there is the little problem of your devoted boyfriend . . . OK, if you're so keen on the truth, Edie, who kisses *you* better, Josh or me? Do you cling to him every time he kisses you? Do you go all soft and shaky when he touches you? 'Cause you do with me.'

It was as if Dylan had been reading this diary. I felt

like he'd cut me open and was looking directly at my heart. I stared out of the window at the French countryside rolling by. Why did I let Dylan break me into tiny pieces just so that he'd have something to do? I could feel one of his fingers tracing little circles on my thigh. I slapped his hand away.

'You know he doesn't,' I managed to choke out. 'He's nice and he's really into me, but he's not you.'

I couldn't look at Dylan but I could feel his eyes boring into me. 'So why are you going out with him?'

'It seemed like a good idea,' I said in a tiny little croak. 'I thought if I went out with him, I'd stop wanting to go out with you. But it hasn't worked. And now he keeps telling me that he's madly in love with me and I feel like a complete bitch. It's all your fault.'

I found the courage to glance up and collided with a look from Dylan that made my stomach flip over.

'So . . . ?' he prompted.

'So, I guess I should stop lying to Josh and dump him. And tell you that I, um, that if you just want a no-strings relationship with me, I reckon I could handle it.'

Dylan was very still, statue still, his whole body tense like he was about to spring up and get as far away from me as humanly possible. 'And what do you mean by a no-strings relationship exactly?'

'I don't know. That we see each other but you, I mean, *we* could see other people. And I wouldn't be all heavy and possessive. I s'pose I could live with that.'

What was I saying? I couldn't live with that. Just 'cause I wanted to be with Dylan didn't mean that I was happy to be some mimsy little creature that let him get up to all kinds with all kinds of other girls just because his kisses turned me inside out. And because he made me feel like the Edie I wanted to be, instead of the Edie that I was. It still wasn't a fair deal.

Dylan wasn't saying anything. I nudged him with my foot.

'Jeez, Dylan, you have to say something.'

He took one of my hands and clutched my fingers really tightly. 'You wouldn't really be happy in a relationship like that,' he said softly. 'You know you wouldn't. I don't know what to say. I've been thinking about you and me a lot. But I don't know . . .'

I waited, with my heart in my mouth and on my sleeve and just about everywhere else, for him to finish the sentence, but he squeezed my hand, let it go and straightened up.

'This is just too heavy. C'mon, let's play the alphabet game again. I went to the festival and I took an antique dinner service dating from the early 1800s . . .'

What a long strange trip it was going to be.

Friday (still!)

I must have fallen asleep at some stage because when I woke up, I realised I was all over Dylan like a bad case of nits. Even worse, my mouth had dropped open and

I'd left a damp patch on the shoulder of his jacket. I didn't even want to think about the possibility of him seeing me dribble. I looked at my watch. It was seven-thirty. We'd been travelling for twelve hours!

I stole a glance at Dylan, but he seemed to be asleep. His eyelashes (oh, why do I always end up transfixed by his eyelashes?) were fluttering gently against his cheeks and his pout of a mouth was relaxed. Even though the coach had slowed down as it wended its way through the narrow Paris streets, Dylan carried on sleeping. Cautiously, so as not to wake him up, I reached towards the floor where my bag was and rummaged inside it until my hand closed around the camera I'd stashed in there. I don't know why, I just wanted a picture of Dylan looking vulnerable. It would make me feel better when I was feeling all down about us not being together. Like, he was just a bog-standard boy or something. I prayed that Dylan wouldn't wake up as I held down the flash and aimed the camera at him.

CLICK! as I pressed the shutter, the flash went off and Dylan came to with a start. I hid the camera down by my side and tried to look dead casual, though I had the feeling that I failed quite spectacularly.

'What was that?' he enquired sleepily.

I feigned wide-eyed innocence. 'What was what?'

Dylan rubbed his face sleepily. 'That flash of light. Was it lightning?' He leaned against me to peer out of the window, which was just enough touch to keep me going for well into the next century. 'Uh, it's not even raining.'

'You must have been dreaming,' I shrugged, as if the conversation wasn't interesting me in the slightest.

'Nah, there was definitely a light.'

I was saved from having to answer as the coach finally came to a halt.

'Oooh, we've reached the hotel,' I cried like it was the most exciting thing that had ever happened. 'Great!'

Dylan collapsed back in his seat. 'I'm shattered,' he grumbled. 'We've been on this bloody coach for, like, ever. And I'm starving. I hope we get to eat soon.'

That's so typical of boys. Dylan and I had shared such an intense time today what with all the face touching on the ferry and that downright horrible conversation about kissing, but now all he seemed to care about was shovelling food into his stomach. I couldn't help looking up to the heavens and sighing.

'What's up with you?' Dylan demanded as he tried to stand up. There were too many people blocking the aisle so he gave up and sat back down next to me.

'Nothing.' What was the use of trying to explain anything to Dylan? He was determined to be denial boy. He was the king of denial. All he wanted to do was pretend that stuff between us was all right when actually it was pretty much screwed up.

Out of the corner of my eye, I could see Dylan

pulling a face at me for being moody but instead of saying anything, he stood up again and managed, this time, to get in the aisle and pull our bags down from the overhead locker. I stood up and surreptitiously shoved the camera back into my vintage Christian Dior shoulder bag, which I got for a steal on eBay and loved, possibly even more than Dylan.

It took ages to get everyone's suitcases out of the coach's boot and sign in at the hotel reception desk. Hôtel Du Lac (literally translated as Hotel Of The Lake, as if there would be a lake in the middle of Paris) was cool in a really old and crumbling kind of way. With its faded cabbage rose wallpaper and over-stuffed red velvet chairs, it looked like it had last been re-decorated sometime in the 1920s. I sat in one of the chairs while Shona went to get our key from Madame La Réceptionniste who looked like she'd been left over from the 1920s too.

'You coming, Eeds?' Shona was standing over me, brandishing the key. I picked up my bags and suitcase and followed her over to the stairs.

Then I stopped.

'What floor are we on again?' I asked.

'Do you want the bad news or the really bad news?'

'What do you mean?'

'We're on the fifth floor and . . . there's no lift,' she told me with a roll of her eyes.

'Great. What a perfect end to a hideous day.'

'I hear you,' Shona said with feeling.

We started climbing up the very steep, very twisty spiral staircase. 'I'm starving. I've had almost nothing to eat today,' I said before I ran out of breath somewhere between the first and second floor.

By the time we reached the fifth floor I was mentally cursing whatever imp of stupidity had forced me to bring a suitcase, a large holdall and a shoulder bag. I never could travel light.

We staggered down a dimly-lit corridor until we came to room 507. Shona was just putting her key in the lock and I was muttering something about how today couldn't get any worse, when the door suddenly swung open to reveal Paul and Mia locked in a clinch on the bed.

'Seems like you spoke too soon,' hissed Shona between gritted teeth. She kicked the door so it crashed against the wall loudly. Mia and Paul looked up. Mia had this horrible sly smile on her face as if she'd known that Shona and I had been standing in the doorway watching. Paul, at least, had the grace to look ashamed.

'Hi, Shona,' he mumbled, scrambling to his feet.

Shona looked at him as if he was a slug that had just crawled out of her salad.

Paul carried on looking at her, almost as if there were things he wanted to say but didn't know how to say them. But Shona stood there, staring at the ceiling. I knew why. I knew that if she spoke to him, she'd burst into tears. I've been there.

I so wasn't in the mood for all this drama. I dropped my bags on the floor and looked pointedly at Paul and then the door.

'You're not sharing with us are you, Paul?' I asked him. I tried to smile to show that I didn't hate him. I mean, Paul had always been really sweet to me before he started going out with Mia. He ran a hand through his hair. 'Nah, I'm in with Dylan and Simon across the corridor. I was just, um, giving Mia a hand with her stuff.'

Mia stretched luxuriously on the bed. 'Thanks sweetie. I guess you'd better go. I'll see you in the lobby in five, OK?'

Now that he'd been officially dismissed, Paul couldn't get out of the door fast enough.

I looked around the room. It was ginormous. I could have fitted my bedroom into it four times over. There was a huge double bed and a single bed plus all this odd, mismatched furniture as well as a telly that should have been in a museum. Mia and Shona were trying to out-stare each other but not saying a word, so I wandered into the en-suite bathroom.

'Oh my God, there's a bidet in there,' I wittered as I came out of the bathroom but Shona and Mia weren't listening. They were too busy arguing.

'. . . No way. There's two of us, you can't expect Edie and I to share a single bed,' Shona was shouting.

Mia smiled that cat-like smile of hers and raised an eyebrow. 'Well, if you wanted to bag the double bed you should have been a little quicker, shouldn't you? But that's always been your problem hasn't it, Shona? You don't know what you want until someone else has it.'

Shona was trying desperately to hang on to her temper. 'I suppose you mean Paul?' she bit out.

'Now why would I talk about *my* boyfriend with you?' enquired Mia nastily.

I was so fed up. It had been such a long day and I didn't have the energy to deal with Mia.

'God, Mia, why do you always have to be such a bitch?' I asked wearily. It was a mistake. Mia turned on me, her pale blue eyes flashing.

'You can shut up, Edie,' she snapped. 'You don't know about anything. You think because Dylan snogs you a couple of times, you're having the romance of the century.'

'No I don't,' I protested, but I didn't sound very convincing.

'Yeah, you do,' said Mia spitefully. 'If you think he'd ever go out with a stupid, flat-chested geek like you . . .'

'Oh, do shut up, Mia.' Shona rolled her eyes.

But Mia wouldn't shut up. 'I mean, Dylan isn't like your dweeby boyfriend Josh. He wants a girl who's into more than just holding hands, if you catch my drift.'

I pounced at Mia, who gave a little scream and ran towards the bathroom. Before I could reach her and strangle her – anything to shut her up – she'd slammed the bathroom door.

'Just calm down, Eeds,' warned Shona, putting a hand on my arm.

I shrugged it off. 'I won't calm down,' I shrieked, bursting into tears. 'If you don't come out, Mia, your stuff's going out the window,' I yelled, kicking the bathroom door.

'You don't have the guts, geek girl,' she taunted.

At that moment I was mad enough to do anything. So I grabbed her bag, opened the window and flung it out.

'You little bitch!' screamed Mia, who'd come out of the bathroom just in time to see her possessions sailing through the air.

The next minute she'd launched herself at me.

It was *on*. Mia was hitting and scratching me. I was whacking her back and Shona was somewhere in the middle of us, trying to break up the fight but just getting Mia's fists in her face.

'What the hell is going on in here?' shouted a voice from the doorway. It was Tania.

Mia and I stopped clawing at each other.

'It was her!' we both said.

'Shona, what's going on?' bellowed Tania, her face all blotchy and shiny.

Shona wound a finger through her hair. 'Mia was being a Grade One bitch,' she explained helpfully.

Mia chose that moment to burst into loud sobs. It was obvious that she was a great fat faker, but it was also obvious that she had a huge red mark on her cheek where I'd belted her.

'They ganged up on me, Tania,' Mia wept. 'They don't want to share a room with me because I'm going out with Shona's ex-boyfriend.'

'Huh! Not even,' I burst out. 'She, I mean, Mia, said . . .' I tailed off. When you're trying to explain to like, a grown-up why you've been fighting you just end up sounding like a petty five-year-old. Anyway, I'd already had one run-in with Tania today.

Then Mia played her joker. 'Edie threw all my stuff out the window,' she announced in a tiny, teary voice.

If there's one thing worse than being bored and depressed, it's being bored and depressed *and* on your own in a foreign hotel. After Mia had grassed on me, Tania gave me this huge lecture about how it had been a really bad idea to let sixteen-year-old A-level students go on a trip with a bunch of nineteen-year-old Foundation Art bods (completely ignoring the fact that Mia was doing A-levels too) and grounded me! Oh, and she'd made me run all the way down the stairs to retrieve Mia's bag before it got run over.

I whinged about how hungry I was and then refused the plate of cheese sandwiches that Tania said I could order from the housekeeper. I hate cheese. I hoped the guilt of leaving me hungry and on my own would make Tania choke on her stupid tofu-burger.

I lay on the bed, half watching this French game show which involved the contestants taking their clothes off. They're very open-minded about that kind of thing on the Continent, but mostly I sulked. OK, I shouldn't have let Mia get to me, but how did she always manage to hit my weak spots? Dylan, Josh and even my breast-size (or complete lack thereof). All the stuff that I'm self-conscious about, Mia went for. She must take lessons on being a bitch, no-one could be born like that.

After Tania had finished reading me the riot act and Mia had sauntered out of the room to meet Paul, Shona had sat on the bed with her arms round me while I cried.

'It's all right, sweetie,' Shona had said comfortingly. And because she'd dropped her usual too cool for school act and didn't come out with any smart remarks, I'd just cried harder.

'It's not fair,' I spluttered.

'What's up?' Oh God, it would have to be Dylan. Our door was still wide open and Dylan was standing in the doorway. 'It sounded like World War Three was going on in here.'

'Just leave it, Dylan,' said Shona. 'I'll be down in a minute.'

But he didn't budge. 'You coming to dinner too, Edie?' he asked.

'Oh, just piss off,' I snarled at him, much to his and Shona's shock.

Dylan gave me a really dirty look and walked away.

'That was way harsh,' commented Shona.

I bit my lip. 'I never swear,' I sobbed. 'Brilliant. Now Dylan hates me.'

'He doesn't hate you,' said Shona with a sigh. 'Look, everyone's out of sorts. It's been a really long day. Do you want me to stay with you?'

I shook my head and insisted that she go with the others, so I could wallow in self-pity like it would be out of fashion by tomorrow.

So, now I was on my own and after I'd spent a bit of time re-living that terrible moment when I'd sworn at Dylan and he'd flung me the filthiest look ever, I concentrated on Mia and how to get my revenge. I couldn't think of any really spectacular act of retribution to avenge me and Shona, but I did spit in her moisturiser and it made me feel a teensy bit better.

A couple of hours had passed and I couldn't sleep. Even though I didn't want to face Mia, I was half hoping that everyone would come back soon. I was so bored. I was mindlessly channel hopping when my phone rang. It was Shona.

'Edie, c'est moi!' said Shona. 'We're on our way home. Do you want anything from Maccy D's?'

I nearly started crying again. Shona could be so sweet. 'Yeah. I want Chicken McNuggets without sauce, and fries and a chocolate milkshake. I'm *so* hungry.'

'Well, you'd have hated dinner anyway.' Shona sounded as if she was smiling. 'Tania made us go to a wholefood vegetarian restaurant. Hang on. Oh, Dylan wants to know if you want a McFlurry as well?'

I held the receiver away from my ear for a second.

'Is Dylan there with you?' I couldn't help asking.

'Yup, but he's just about to go on a mercy dash to McDonald's for you,' Shona said, before lowering her voice. 'He had a go at Tania in front of everyone for sending you to bed without any dinner.'

'So he's forgiven me for swearing at him?' I was almost giddy with hope.

'Oh you've got me to thank for that,' said Shona breezily. 'I explained to him about young girls and their hormones.'

'Gee, Shona, you're a real pal,' I said sarcastically.

'Less of the lip, young lady. Anyway, gotta go, see you in about ten minutes.'

Isn't that always the way? Just when you think that life sucks with added bits of sucking, the boy of your dreams is fighting your battles for you and buying you McFlurries. And I couldn't help but hope that maybe there was a very, very slim chance that Dylan and I could . . .

Saturday

I'd slept like the dead. Even though Shona took up most of the bed and tried to steal the blankets, I'd fallen asleep the minute my head had touched the rather lumpy pillow. I was just glad that Mia hadn't won the battle of the beds, because if we'd been in that single one, Shona would have had me on the floor. She sure takes up a lot of room when she's asleep. I was woken up from a strange dream about kissing Tom Hardy while we were both trapped in a mineshaft by the bleeping of my travel clock.

'Turn it off,' whimpered Shona, burrowing deeper under the bedclothes.

I nudged her with my foot. Repeatedly. In a very annoying way. 'It's eight o'clock, I don't want to miss breakfast.'

Shona made an unimpressed grunting noise and snatched the covers away from me so I had no choice but to actually get up. Mia was still asleep. She hadn't come back with Shona but must have crept into the room after we'd crashed out.

By the time I emerged from the bathroom, Shona was up and rummaging through my suitcase.

'Did you pack the dress with the cherries on it?' she asked. I loved seeing Shona first thing in the morning. Her usually poker straight black hair was sticking up and she was wearing pink pyjamas with rabbits on them. If anyone saw her, her icy cool image would be shot to smithereens.

'I don't think so,' I said. 'I think I stuck to a muted colour palette.'

I started drying my hair and hoped that the noise would wake up Mia but she was still out for the count. Shona disappeared into the bathroom and I dithered about what to wear.

I'm not one of those sad girls who always dresses to attract boys, but knowing that I was going to spend the whole day in close proximity to Dylan made it hard to decide on the right outfit. In the end, I chose my new Nordic-style sweater dress which I loved with a fiery passion, black woolly tights and a skinny, striped scarf. It was a pretty stylin' ensemble, even if I do say it myself.

'Nice outfit,' commented Shona. 'Did you pack your black skinny jeans?'

Shona, on the other hand, takes ages getting dressed.

'I'm not going to spend half an hour watching you try on all my clothes,' I told her with a smile. 'I'll see you later.'

'Save me a croissant,' she said as she started burrowing once more in my suitcase.

As I skipped down the spiral staircase, I felt much happier. I was in Paris! My parents were miles away and Dylan was being an absolute sweetheart. He wouldn't even let me pay for the McDonald's last night and when I'd tried to apologise for swearing at him, he'd been his most charming.

'Oh, forget it, Edie,' he'd said lightly. 'It's not the first time someone's sworn at me.'

'Yeah, and it probably won't be the last,' Shona had added caustically before shutting the door in his face, as I all but dived headfirst into my Chicken McNuggets.

I walked across the hotel foyer and was trying to remember where the dining room was when I realised that Tania was bearing down on me.

I'd decided last night that I'd really got off on the wrong foot with her and that I should try and behave when she was around. But I still thought that she should wear a bra.

'Hi Tania,' I said politely. 'I just wanted to say that I'm sorry about yesterday.'

Tania looked a bit thrown. 'Well, that's OK, I'm . . .'

'Look I know we didn't get off to a good start,' I continued. 'But I hope we can forget about all that.'

She gave my arm a little squeeze and beamed at me. Sucker!

'Edie, I'm terribly sorry about last night. I was very pre-menstrual, I should never have stopped you from coming out to dinner,' she puffed.

In other words, please don't tell your parents that I tried to starve you.

'Well, that's all right,' I said in a small voice. 'Though I am really hungry. I couldn't sleep last night 'cause my tummy kept rumbling.'

That wiped the tree-hugging smile off her face. 'Well, we need to get some breakfast inside you,' she decided and frogmarched me off to the dining room.

I was all set to go over to Nat and Trent but Tania had other ideas. She hustled me over to the breakfast buffet and tried to insist that I had a glass of milk because I looked 'really peaky and young girls need a lot of calcium to make their bones strong'.

'I only drink milk when it's got chocolate powder in it,' I protested. 'I want white toast with lots of butter, coffee and an apple.'

'That's not enough to keep you going,' Tania said bossily. 'Do you have an eating disorder? You're very pasty.'

Oh God, she was a nightmare. I finally managed to persuade her that I wasn't anorexic or suffering from some fatal strain of anaemia and she let me go. Dylan was already pulling out a chair for me and though I wanted to spend some quality hanging-out time with Nat and Trent, I walked slowly over to the table Dylan was sharing with Simon and Paul.

'What was all that about?' asked Simon as I put down my toast.

I rolled my eyes. 'She's terrified that I'm going to tell my 'rents that she deprived me of dinner and then she started going on about eating disorders and the four major food groups and how breakfast is the most important meal of the day. What's up with you?'

There was some major smirking going on between the three of them. It was very annoying.

Paul indicated a big pink envelope. 'The receptionist asked us to give this to you.'

I opened it and my heart sank. It was a card from Josh wishing me Bonnes Vacances and telling me how much he'd miss me. I'd only been gone for twenty-four hours and I'd texted him last night. I shoved it under the placemat and started buttering my toast.

'He obviously loves his big romantic gestures then,' Dylan muttered.

'It's a lovely, thoughtful gesture,' I said stoutly.

Dylan looked sheepish. 'Ah. Well if that's how you feel, Edie, what can I say?'

'How about not saying anything?' I snapped, but it's quite hard to pull off icy indignation when you've got a mouthful of toast.

Dylan looked at me as if I was a really cryptic crossword clue.

I raised my eyebrows. 'What?'

'I just don't get it,' he said, shrugging his shoulders. 'What satisfaction can you get from stringing him along like this?'

'What are you talking about?' I spat out furiously. I was dimly aware of Simon and Paul muttering their goodbyes and getting up hastily.

'Well, he's obviously totally crazy about you. I mean, he made sure that card was waiting for you and it's also obvious that you don't give a stuff about him.'

I couldn't believe that Dylan would turn on me like this. OK, Josh was way more into me than I was into him, but Dylan knew why I was going out with Josh. And he knew how bad I felt about it. So why was he trying to make me feel even worse?

I didn't say any of this to Dylan. He was staring out of the window, the weak morning light hitting his face so he was all planes and angles. He seemed really cold and unapproachable.

I pushed my plate away – I'd suddenly lost my appetite – and scraped my chair back noisily as I stood up. Dylan looked at me questioningly.

'I don't have to listen to this, Dylan,' I bit out. 'And I don't know why you're getting so upset on Josh's behalf, he's never bothered you before.'

Dylan reached across the table and gripped my wrist tightly so I couldn't pull away.

'You know why he's bothering me,' he said and then lowered his voice when he realised that people were turning round to look at us. 'Sort it out.'

I managed to free my wrist and tried to stalk out of the dining room with some semblance of dignity. I decided to go for a walk. I needed fresh air and I needed some time to try and work out what the hell Dylan was on.

But I'd only been walking for about five seconds when I realised that the Hôtel Du Lac was situated in Pigalle. And that Pigalle is the red-light district of Paris. I was so busy goggling at posters featuring busty women in their smalls and neon signs that promised, 'Girls, Girls, Girls!' that, to be honest, I completely forgot about Dylan. Mum and Dad were gonna freak when I told them about this!

We were meant to be meeting in the foyer at ten to go to the Louvre, but hardly anybody was there. I finally managed to hook up with Nat and Trent who made room for me on one of the sofas.

'What's going on?'

Trent nudged me playfully. 'Exactly what we were going to ask you.'

'Yeah, what was that scene with you and Dylan at breakfast?' added Nat.

'Huh! He's gone down with a severe case of boy disease,' I snorted. 'I think it could be fatal this time. Anyway, where is everyone?'

Nat squeezed his eyes tight and stretched like he does when he's got juicy gossip. '*Weeelllll*, Shona and Paul have disappeared off the face of the earth, Mia's gone back to bed in a strop, Dylan and Simon have decided to make their own way to the Louvre even though the only thing they can say in French is something very, very rude and half the boys in the Foundation class have realised that we're in the middle of the red-light area and gone to a strip show.'

'I know about *that*,' I said witheringly, so neither of them thought that I was completely clueless when it came to information gathering. 'I just saw them go into a club called The Pink Pussycat.'

'Boys are *so* sad,' commented Trent.

'I couldn't agree more,' I said sourly.

The day wasn't a dead loss. The six of us who were still around and Martyn (Tania, thank the Lord, had gone to meet some of her hippy friends) went to a proper French café for cappuccinos and then braved the Metro. My A-level French made me the star of the hour. Everyone was dead impressed as I approached the ticket office and recited, '*Excusez-moi, monsieur, je voudrais sept billets Louvre, s'il vous plaît.*'

Outside the Louvre was this weird glass pyramid thingy that I wanted to take pictures of, so Nat and Trent waited patiently while I fiddled around with my camera and evil-eyed any inconsiderate people who had the audacity to walk across my line of vision.

Once we actually got inside, we decided to kick it free style. Following a tour guide round and listening to them blithering on about 'the textural qualities of

Van Gogh's later work' is the exact opposite of fun. Instead, Nat, Trent and me spent half an hour pretending that I was a stinking rich jetsetter who wanted to buy some pictures to go in my New York penthouse and Nat was my personal assistant and Trent was this really oily gallery owner who had to suck up to me 'cause I was so shockingly, obscenely wealthy. Sometimes I find it hard to believe that I'm nearly seventeen, I can be very immature.

The most famous painting in the Louvre is the Mona Lisa but when we got to it; actually not so much. It's really small and dark and it's covered in bullet-proof glass which makes the light reflect on the picture so you can't get a proper look at it.

The three of us stood in a line in front of the picture and tried to see if her eyes really did follow you around like they were supposed to.

'And this is one of our most legendary exhibits, madam,' said Trent. 'Does madam care for it?'

I wrinkled my nose.

'I don't think madam does care for it,' said Nat.

I pulled a face. 'It doesn't match my colour scheme. Have you got something that's a bit less green?'

'Oh yes, madam and I really aren't feeling the green,' chimed in Nat.

Eventually we got bored playing and Nat and Trent went off to find some statue of a naked bloke so I wandered about on my own. I didn't really rate the pictures that much. They were all dark and gloomy or full of chubby-faced cherubs and topless women.

I was just watching some art boy (not one of ours) who was working on an amazing reproduction of one of the Old Masters when I felt a pair of hands creep round my waist and someone kiss the back of my neck. I knew it was Dylan. All my insides turned to mush.

I turned around and he cupped my face and gave me the lightest kiss on the mouth. It was the merest whisper. A prelude to a kiss. The art boy winked at me as Dylan took my hand and started pulling me through all these inter-connecting rooms but everything was a blur around me. The only thing I was sure of was Dylan's hand clasped in mine. It was right that we didn't speak. Speaking would have ruined the spell that seemed to have woven itself around us when he'd come up behind me.

We ended up in this small anteroom off the main drag. There was no-one else in it, apart from a security guard who was asleep in his chair. Dylan and I looked deep into each other's eyes and for a moment there were no secrets or lies or Mia or Josh between us. We were just Dylan and Edie and we were the only people left in the world.

Then we were both reaching for each other and Dylan had backed me against the wall and he was kissing me hard. Harder than he'd ever kissed me before. But I was kissing him back with just as much fervour. His hands were under my denim jacket and I wasn't even freaking out about where they were going. I was aware of so many things. Of the sleeping security guard. Of the hum of the lights and the faint whirr of the air conditioning. Of Dylan's heart beating really fast. And the feel of his body as he pressed me against the wall. Of the way I was standing on tiptoe so he could reach my mouth. And especially of the way our mouths clung together and the feel of his tongue against mine and the faint scrape of his teeth as he nibbled my bottom lip.

When we came up for air, I carried on leaning back against the wall so I didn't fall over. One of Dylan's hands was still inside my jacket as he stroked the curve of my waist and kissed my ear and my neck and the little knobbly bits between my collar bones. We still didn't speak. Then we were kissing again and his hands were in my hair and I was clutching greedy handfuls of his leather jacket. We broke off again as we both became aware of the sound of voices getting nearer. I took in a couple of deep lungfuls of air. Dylan was all flushed and breathing hard like he'd run a marathon. He looked like he was going to say something but just as a group of tourists arrived in our little room he bent his head, stole one last swift kiss and sauntered away.

Saturday, but later
I felt completely dazed. So dazed, that when Nat and Trent found me I was sat dreamy-faced on a bench.

'What's up with you?' asked Nat.

'Yeah, you look really weird,' added Trent peering at my face.

I tried to act normally but I was completely spaced out. All I could do was gingerly prod my lips, which felt all tingly and sore from where they'd been melded onto Dylan's mouth.

On the Metro back to the hotel, I still didn't speak. I just kept re-playing the whole thing back in my head from when Dylan had come up behind me to that last, devastating kiss he'd pressed onto me before exiting stage right.

Shona was waiting for me in the foyer. I'd been planning on having a long, soaky bath so I could go over the kissing a few more hundred times but Shona was, like, you outside, now.

'What's your damage?' I protested as she pulled me bodily around the revolving door and out into the street.

'The walls have ears,' she said cryptically.

'What?'

'It's not official or anything but Paul and I are . . . on,' she informed me smugly.

'Define "on",' I said, smiling vaguely at Martyn as he passed us on the street.

Shona's mouth twisted. 'Back together. Exclusively. No more skanky maybe girlfriends lurking in the background.' And the way she fisted her hands against her sides told me more than her throwaway tone. I was confused because last night Paul had seemed quite happy to be sucking face with his skanky maybe girl-friend. 'So how did you manage that?'

'I sat him down and told him that I was done moping around after him. That I was over him and I'd moved on . . .'

'Which isn't even remotely true,' I pointed out.

She pulled a face at me. 'I hate it when you start being all perceptive, so cut it out right now.'

'And then what happened?' I wanted to know.

'Well, he didn't say anything for a while and then he squinched up his face like he was in pain and said that he didn't want me to move on because he wasn't ready to move on.' She rolled her eyes like it was no big deal but I knew it was. I'd seen her face whenever Paul and Mia were in the same room and she looked like her whole world had turned to broken biscuit.

I leaned against the wall and gave her a look to let her know I was on to her. 'And then?' I prompted.

'I just told him that if he was going to be my boyfriend then I wasn't going to stand for any more of his nonsense. It was quite easy really.'

I was still having trouble understanding all this.

'But I thought you'd split up . . .'

'Nah, we were just taking a break,' explained Shona impatiently. 'It was all going really quickly. It's not like you and Dylan. Within two days of Dylan introducing me and Paul we were having a serious thing. And I needed more time to think things through.'

'Before you slept with him, you mean,' I interrupted.

Shona shrugged. 'Well, it's a big step to take. I wanted to be really sure about Paul before I made that kind of commitment. And he has got a lot of stuff to make up to me before we get to that step again.'

'I guess that makes sense. He doesn't deserve to get your goodies right away,' I said. 'So, what about Mia?'

'What about her?' snapped Shona. 'She's history, she just doesn't know that she's history. Yet.'

'But I thought she and Paul . . .'

'Well, you thought wrong, hon,' Shona said in a kinder voice. 'Paul and I were only meant to be having a bit of a breather and, next thing I know, Mia's telling everyone that we've split up because Paul's in love with her! She can't resist other girls' boyfriends. I mean, she never fancied Dylan until he started going out with Lilah.'

'Lilah? That girl who runs the college magazine?' My heart sank. Lilah was blonde, gorgeous and really, really smart.

'Hey, remember to breathe, now she's going out with the guy in that stupid band we saw a few weeks ago. What are they called? The Swimsuits . . .'

'Bikini Dust,' I muttered. 'So was Dylan really into her?'

Shona rolled her eyes. 'I wish I hadn't said

anything. It was over ages ago and he couldn't have been that into her or he wouldn't have started fooling around with Mia.'

I felt slightly better. 'I don't know what they all see in her.'

'She's got big tits and she puts out,' Shona said with a wicked smile.

'Shona!'

'Well, it's true,' she grinned. 'So are you cool about me and Paul?'

I nodded.

'And you're not going to go up to our room and get depressed about Lilah?'

I shook my head.

'And are you going to tell me where you got that shocking lovebite from?'

'Wouldn't you like to know?' I shrieked before running back into the hotel.

Mia was in the room, sifting through her clothes. Sometimes I think that if you added up all the hours that girls spend looking through their wardrobes each year, you'd have enough time to find a solution to global warming.

I was still hell bent on getting in the bath and I didn't really want to have anything to do with Mia and I guess she felt the same way too, but I couldn't help feeling sorry for her. I mean, she was like the poster girl for low self-esteem, hence the constantly chasing after boys, like their approval was the only important thing in her world. And she didn't know that Paul was about to dump her and, when I thought about it, I realised that she didn't really have any friends. Then she looked up and sneered at me and I stopped feeling sorry for her.

When I got out of the bath and wandered into the bedroom with a towel wrapped round me, I was a bit freaked out to see Shona, Nat and Trent perched on the bed.

'You took your time, kid,' said Shona mock-indignantly, almost knocking me into the wall as she rushed into the bathroom.

'We're going to a club after dinner,' Nat informed me. 'Martyn says that he doesn't care what we get up to as long as we don't get arrested by the gendarmerie.'

'I'm never going to get into a club,' I moaned. 'I can't even pass for eighteen.'

Nat and Trent thought differently. I swear to God, when I'm rich and famous, I'm going to employ them as my stylists. Half an hour later, I was wearing Shona's long, silky black Chinese dress with the slits up the side, my hair was twisted and pinned up and the glitter on my face made me look all eyes and cheekbones.

'Edie, you are *not* wearing your Converses,' protested Trent. 'I forbid it.'

'No, the Converses are OK,' insisted Nat. 'Any other footwear would just be too much.'

'Thank you,' I said pointedly as I pulled on my pink sneakers. 'Don't start arguing,' I added warningly to Trent.

'Dylan is gonna lose it when he sees you,' exclaimed Shona gleefully, emerging from the bathroom. 'He won't know where to put himself.'

I paused midway through applying another coat of Cherry Bomb lip-stain.

'I'm not dressing up like this for Dylan,' I protested. 'It's so I can get into a nightclub.'

'Yeah, right!'

'Whatever!'

'Yuh-ha!'

Sometimes I violently dislike my friends.

Martyn had booked the longest table in the world in this poky French restaurant. I loved it. The walls were covered in leopard skin and had little gold cherubs and red fairylights strung everywhere. Sort of like a distressed fairy grotto.

Shona was trying to subtly organise the seating (which meant that she told Simon to get up off his arse 'or I'll kill you') so Dylan and I were sitting next to each other and her and Paul were opposite. There was one hairy moment when it looked like Mia was going to foul things up but just as she was about to plant her butt in my seat, Martyn called her over and wanted to know why she'd spent the morning in bed instead of soaking up the Parisian culture.

Although the table was long, there were a lot of us and it was a bit of a squash. I could feel Dylan looking at me but I felt inexplicably shy and awkward, probably because last time I'd seen him he'd been kissing me into the wall. It might also have had something to do with his leg pressing against me. I re-adjusted the slit in my dress so I wasn't flashing a large amount of thigh and then started rearranging my cutlery. I always fidget like mad when I get nervous. Luckily, Nat was sitting on the other side of me.

'You'll have to translate the menu for me, Edie,' he said plaintively. 'It's all in French.'

'I know it's a crazy notion, but that might have something to do with us being in France,' Trent pointed out from across the table.

'Do you speak French?' Dylan suddenly asked me.

I started to say something idiotic about my French A-level, when I heard Nat hiss at Trent, 'Only with her tongue!' and I collapsed into hysterical giggles.

'Are you on crack?' Dylan enquired, raising one of his eyebrows like I was the most amusing thing he'd seen all year.

I shook my head. 'No . . . It's nothing, Nat just said something funny.'

Dylan moved even nearer to me, if that was at all

possible. He smelt of lemon verbena and washing powder and it made me feel lightheaded. 'I thought about you all afternoon,' he whispered in my ear. 'I think my heart's still racing.'

I knew I was blushing. Did I say blushing? What I actually meant was my face was doing a good impersonation of a pillar box.

'Don't go all shy on me,' drawled Dylan. 'You look really cool tonight. Not that you don't normally.' His voice suddenly shifted off the sultry setting. 'Anyway, can you understand, like, any of the stuff on this menu?'

I managed to gain control of myself somehow and spent the next fifteen minutes translating the menu. Simon was persuading people to order disgusting stuff like snails and Nat and Trent decided that if people wouldn't eat it, they'd have to do a dare instead but I stuck with a plain omelette and chips.

There was a bit of an awkward moment over the drinks. Like, most of the art students are nineteen so they get to drink beer and wine but Tania wasn't very happy about the idea of Mia and me being near so much alcohol. I told her that Mum and Dad have been letting me drink watered-down wine since I was twelve, and after a little sulking from me and some shouty persuasion from the others she gave in.

While we waited for our food to come, Dylan talked to me in a low voice about some paintings he'd seen in the Louvre by an artist called Titian. All the time he had his hand on my leg, just above my knee. Not in a sleazy way, but it was getting harder to concentrate on what he was saying. His voice was just this pleasing hum in my ear, and his body was turned towards me. It seemed like my whole being was centred on the warmth of his hand on my leg. Then his finger started tracing a path along the edge of the slit in my dress. The very high slit in my dress. I wriggled in my chair and Dylan put his hand back above my knee. I still wasn't really listening to what he was saying. I took another sip of my unwatery wine – it really had gone straight to my head.

'I want to kiss you so much . . .'

'What?' I gasped. Then looked around quickly to see if anyone had heard.

Dylan gave me a measured look. 'All I can think about is when I'm going to get to snog you again.'

I giggled nervously. I can be such a *girl* at times.

'Have I embarrassed you?' he said softly.

'Sort of.'

Dylan shifted in his chair and then put his arm around my shoulders. In front of everyone! And all I wanted to do was rest my head in the warm place where his neck met his shoulder and stay there forever.

'I was just wondering.' He paused for a moment. 'I don't suppose you could, um, go and powder your nose. I could meet you outside the Ladies and then we could have another session. You're driving me mad.'

'Dylan! Stop it. I thought we were just meant to be friends.'

He gave me another one of his looks. Really he should patent them; he'd earn a fortune. 'Yeah, well, we can be friends who kiss each other.'

I was saved by our food arriving, but I'd lost my appetite. I poked at my omelette with my fork, while everyone else was making a big deal about the snails, which had turned up in this bile-green sauce. It took precisely thirty-seven seconds (I know because I counted them) before Nat started giving out dares.

Most of the art boys' forfeits seemed to consist of downing glasses of beer in one. I nibbled on a chip and hoped that no-one would notice me.

'Edie, you can't have omelette and chips in a French restaurant,' Simon suddenly announced.

'Yes I can!' I said indignantly. 'It's like a French omelette and French chips. French fries even!'

'Dare! Dare! Dare!' Nat and Trent started chanting. They were going to be coming home in a jam jar if they kept that up.

'OK, I'll do a stupid dare,' I muttered when the chanting got louder. 'But I'm not downing any alcohol in one. And I'm not doing anything that involves food that I don't like.'

'Hmmm, that kind of rules out most things,' said Simon.

'You've got to kiss the person sitting on your right,' Paul suddenly declared to loud cheers from everyone. And, of course, there was something entirely Dylan-shaped sitting on my right.

I made my sad bunny face at Shona but she just raised her glass at me. After I'd killed Nat and Trent, Shona was next on the list.

Dylan slouched back on his chair and curled his tongue behind his front teeth. 'You chicken then?'

I wasn't going to let him get away with that. I leaned forward, grabbed his face and gave him a long, slow kiss on the mouth. Dylan's whole body went rigid but just as he relaxed and opened his mouth, I pulled away to loud applause.

I glanced at Dylan from under my lashes. He was running an unsteady hand through his hair but when he caught my eye, he licked his lips and looked like he wanted to have me for dessert. It was strangely unsettling.

The rest of the meal wasn't so exciting, although from the venomous looks that Mia was shooting in Shona's direction, I had a horrible feeling it was all going to kick off later.

Anyway, like Nat had said, Martyn was cool about us going on to a club. Tania wasn't. She wanted Mia and me to go back to the hotel with her and Martyn. For once, I was with Mia all the way.

'Look, it's not fair,' Mia yelled. 'I go to clubs all the time at home.'

'Me too,' I added. 'I'm not going to drink anything, I just want to have a dance.'

'I have a responsibility to your parents,' said Tania pompously. 'I can't let two underage girls wander round dubious nightspots on their own.'

'But we won't be on our own,' I pointed out.

'I'll keep an eye on Edie,' Shona said. 'I know her parents and they trust me. I can't speak for Mia, though.'

'Well, if Edie's going to a club, then I am too,' argued Mia.

'Fine,' said Tania wearily. 'But I want you back at the hotel by midnight. Don't make Martyn have to come and get you.'

'Thank you, thank you, thank you,' I beamed. 'And I promise I won't be any trouble.'

She didn't seem very convinced.

We ended up in a club called Les Inrockuptibles. It was small and smoky with scruffy little booths around a tiny dancefloor. Dylan was talking to a group of his art boy buds and occasionally glancing over at me when a genuine French garçon asked me to dance! I stayed on the dancefloor for ages, dancing to Les Beatles and some groovy French stuff from the Sixties. Stéphane introduced me to his friends who spoke bad English to me and I spoke bad French to them, but we seemed to understand each other. Vive la différence!

Stéphane bought me un Coca-Cola light and I led him over to the booth where Shona and Paul were sitting.

'This is Stéphane,' I said. 'He's French.'

'Hi. Bye,' shouted Shona over the music. 'I'm going to the bar.'

Paul, Stéphane and I were having a slightly stilted three-way conversation about pop music, with me translating for both of them, when Mia sauntered over and slid into the empty space next to Paul.

'I want a word with you,' she said ominously.

'Um, I thought you might.' Paul looked extremely uncomfortable.

I started to tell Stéphane about what was going on with Shona, Paul and Mia while I tried to keep one ear on what Paul and Mia were saying.

'Shona est très triste,' I was saying. 'Maintenant, Paul et Shona embrassez, er, beaucoup.'

Stéphane was looking dead confused; my tenses were going all over the place.

'Look, Mia, you know I've always loved Shona,' I heard Paul say. 'I've never stopped wanting to be with her.'

'All right, all right,' Mia replied. 'But I still want to be friends with you, Paul, I really care about you. I don't want you to get hurt.'

'Mia est une grande vache,' I told Stéphane.

Mia got up. 'You know where to find me if you need me,' she said sweetly before walking off.

Paul gave a sigh of relief and looked at me hopefully. 'That went surprisingly well,' he commented.

'Yeah, too flaming well,' I added. 'She's up to something.'

Paul shook his head. 'I know you and Mia don't get on but she can be quite caring.'

I snorted in disbelief, which I realise with hindsight isn't the nicest noise to make in front of reasonably attractive boys.

Stéphane touched my arm. 'Edie, I 'ave to return to my friends,' he said in his cute French accent. 'I will see you later for more dancing, yes?'

'Yeah,' I smiled. 'I'll come and find you.'

'I can see you've pulled.' Shona was back with the drinks. 'How did it go with Mia?'

'Fine,' said Paul. 'I told you she'd be cool with it.'

'Yeah, right,' muttered Shona. 'You can be so dumb sometimes, Paul.'

I started sliding out of the booth, I didn't want to have to hear Paul and Shona's first, post-getting-back-together fight.

'And where do you think you're going, missy?' Shona asked. 'What are you doing chatting up young French men when you're meant to be besotted with Dylan?'

'Shona!' I growled. 'I'm going out with Josh. And I was just practising my French and I am so not, as you charmingly put it, besotted with Dylan. We're just friends. We're just doing the friend thing and . . .'

'Edie, you little fibber! What was that tongue thing back in the restaurant?' Paul spluttered. I could see that him and Shona getting back together was not necessarily a good thing. Like, now there'd be two of them ganging up on me.

'I'm not going to dignify that remark with a response,' I said grandly and flounced off to the toilet.

The ladies' toilet was full of foxy French girls being sophisticated and well, French. I fought my way to the mirror and applied some more lip-stain. Usually I'm dead pale but I had a flush to my cheeks from the dancing and my eyes looked huge in my face. I looked quite womanly and as I usually manage to resemble a twelve-year-old, that was really saying something.

As I came out of the loo, Dylan was leaning against the wall. He was all angles and tousled hair. My insides seemed to melt away to nothing. I walked over to him as if he'd telepathically ordered me to.

'I've been looking for you,' he told me with the merest hint of a smile. 'Who's the French boy?'

'Oh, you mean Stéphane? He's cute, isn't he?'

Dylan glowered at me.

I couldn't help myself. 'You wouldn't be jealous,

would you? 'Cause, like, friends don't get jealous when their friends pull cute French boys.'

'No, I'm not jealous,' Dylan all but snarled. 'I was worried about you. He could be Paris's most successful serial killer for all you know.'

I really didn't want to laugh. It would only encourage him. 'Hardly,' I said. 'Oh go on, admit it, you were jealous.'

Dylan shrugged. 'Well, maybe just a little bit.' Now there was a definite and easily recognisable smile playing around his lips.

'So . . .' I said, half turning in the direction of the main room. 'D'you fancy a . . . EEEEEP!'

Dylan had suddenly snaked his hands round my waist and was lifting me onto a pile of crates that were stacked in the corridor where we were standing.

'What did you do that for?' I asked him in a squeaky voice.

'So I won't get neck ache when I kiss you,' he said with a leer.

I gulped. 'Are you gonna kiss me then?'

'Yup.'

Our faces were completely level for once. Dylan was standing so close to me that nothing could have come between us, but he didn't kiss me. Our lips were almost touching and I could feel his breath on my mouth. We stayed like that for a second and then with a groan I reached for him.

I could have died from his kisses. I wrapped my legs around his and pressed myself tight against him as his tongue danced inside my mouth. One of his hands was stroking my leg and my fingers were clutching at his hair.

At one point, as we came up for air, he said softly, 'I don't ever want this to stop,' before he captured my mouth again.

It all started to get really heavy. I was pushed right back against the wall and I could feel Dylan's heart racing against my chest and his hand inching further and further up my thigh. With a great effort, I pulled away slightly. Dylan started to nibble lightly at my bottom lip.

'What's the matter,' he whispered.

'You're going too fast,' I whispered back. 'I think we should stop.'

'Just one more kiss,' Dylan muttered, stroking a hand down my hot face.

'This is all wrong,' I told him breathily. Why couldn't I have just kept my big mouth shut? OK, it might be wrong for about a million reasons but right now I was in Dylan's arms and that was all that really mattered.

'I don't care,' Dylan said and started kissing me again, but he kept his hands on my shoulders and stopped pushing against me. I lost all track of the time, I wasn't aware of anything but Dylan's mouth wreaking havoc on my nervous system when I suddenly realised that something was tugging at my hand. I tried to shake it off but then I was yanked off the crates and only Dylan's hands catching me round my waist stopped me falling.

'Edie! We're going now,' snapped Shona, grabbing my hand. 'Time to say bye to the nice art boy.'

'She's fine where she is,' Dylan insisted, shooting Shona a meaningful look.

'That's what I'm worried about,' said Shona pointedly. 'I've got your coat and bag, let's go.'

'But I don't want to go,' I whined as Shona started dragging me down the corridor. 'I want to stay here.'

'Tough! You're going.'

'I'll come back with you,' decided Dylan, following us back into the club.

'That won't be necessary, thanks,' Shona told him, pulling me towards the door with her horrible freaky strength from swimming three times a week. I dug my heels in but it was no good. She'd have dislocated my shoulder if I hadn't kept up with her. 'Maybe you should have some water, Dylan, you look like you need to cool down.'

Dylan looked puzzled. 'I don't want a drink.'

Shona tugged open the street door and pushed me through it. 'I wasn't talking about drinking it, dumbass,' she threw back at Dylan.

Saturday, but even later
'What did you do that for?' I demanded of Shona. She was still holding my hand and pulling me along the

street. Her lips were all tight, which was never a good sign.

'You should be thanking me,' she said, sounding really angry. 'God knows what would have happened if I hadn't been there.'

'Nothing would have happened. It was fine. I was in control.'

'It didn't look like either of you were in control.'

'Well I was. I told him to slow down.'

Shona came to a halt. 'Look, I don't want you to get hurt,' she said gently. 'Don't get too involved in this weird thing with Dylan.'

She really knew how to kill the mood, did Shona. It was all right when I was with Dylan and he was kissing me but when I wasn't with him, it was easy to see what a mess I'd got myself into. Especially with her around to draw a diagram.

'It's too late for that,' I muttered.

'Oh, c'mon, let's go and have a cup of coffee.' Shona put her arm round me. 'I think there's a café in the next street.'

I went to the counter and ordered two coffees and glanced over at Shona. She was idly tracing patterns with her finger on the table-top and giving a good impression of a girl with terminal PMS.

'What's up?' I asked, as I put the cups down. 'This isn't just about me and Dylan is it?'

Shona gave a deep sigh. 'You know how you can want something for ages, but when you get it, you're not sure if you really do want it? Like, you've spent so much time thinking about how to get it that you forget about what it would really be like to have it?'

'You're talking about Paul, yeah?'

'Yeah,' Shona gave another sigh. 'D'you think I'm stupid to take him back?'

I thought about it. Sure, Shona had been really unhappy when Paul started seeing Mia but she wasn't particularly chuffed now that they were back together either. And how could she trust a boy who starts seeing another girl the minute that they've agreed to have some time out?

'You're right,' agreed Shona obviously reading my mind. 'I don't trust him, not one bit.'

'So how are you going to deal with it?'

Shona threw me her slyest smile. 'I've given him a one-strike deal. No second chances, no explanations. The minute that Paul steps out of line, he's history. I'm not putting up with any more of his crap.'

'I wish I could be as strong as you. I'm such a pushover where boys are concerned.'

'You mean Dylan?' commented Shona, who seemed to rapidly be regaining her normal composure. 'It's weird. You lose all powers of reason when he's about.'

'Oh, don't start . . .' I groaned. I could tell by the steely glint in her eye that Shona was going to have the Dylan thing out with me. Without an anaesthetic.

'No, Edie, I'm serious, I really want to know why he has this, this . . . *hold* on you. I mean, I just don't get it. Like, it's *Dylan.*'

'Of course you don't understand,' I told her crossly. 'You've known him forever, you played in sandpits together at nursery school blah blah blah, repeat to fade.'

'Yeah and I know exactly what he's like,' laughed Shona. 'Don't get me wrong, I love him to bits, but that doesn't mean that I'm blind to his many, many faults. He's moody, he's insecure, he's secretive . . .'

'. . . he's ruthless, he's manipulative,' I continued for her. 'Like, he engineers these confrontations so I'm all upset and vulnerable and then he kisses me. And when I'm with him, I have this sick feeling of excitement in my tummy like I'm about to jump off a diving board or something. I never feel relaxed when Dylan's around. But, at the same time, being with him feels so *right.* You don't know how confused I am.'

'I'm starting to,' said Shona with a serious look on her face. 'You've got it bad.'

'I know,' I said sadly. 'And I don't think he'll ever go out with me. Not ever and I don't understand why.'

Shona reached across the table and touched my hand. 'I know that he thinks the world of you, Edie. And, don't take this the wrong way, but sometimes I wonder whether you're his type.'

It felt like the whole of my world had just collapsed. 'I don't want to hear this, I don't want to know.'

'Look, I'm your friend,' Shona insisted. 'I have to say this to you because I don't want you to get hurt and I think that Dylan needs the kind of girl who can look after herself and who can keep him in line.'

'Like Lilah?'

'Well, at least she didn't let Dylan get away with murder,' Shona said brutally. 'She wasn't the type of girl who'd sit around and get depressed because Dylan was in one of his moods or because he hadn't called when he said he would and she wouldn't let him play his weird little mind games with her.'

'I, um . . . I don't . . . I wouldn't either,' I said in a tiny voice, because I knew that it wasn't true.

Shona rolled her eyes. 'Edie, could you be any more delusional?' she snorted. 'What was going on in the club? Dylan knows that you're going out with Josh and he knows that the two of you are meant to be just friends, so why do you think he keeps putting the moves on you? Because you let him! You've got to stop it. And you've got to do something about Josh. Either make a go of it or put the poor lad out of his misery but stop stringing him along. It's just not fair, hon.'

Shona might as well have poured a bucket of cold water over me. Again. Everything that she'd said was right. It was just super hard to admit it to myself.

'OK, I'm going to finish with Josh when we get home,' I announced decisively. 'I'm not being fair on him.'

Shona gave my hand a little squeeze. 'And what are you going to do about Dylan?'

'Stop kissing him?'

'Are you asking me or are you telling me?' Shona wanted to know but I wasn't sure so I made my second sad bunny face of the evening and there ain't no weapon forged that can defeat its power. Even Shona got the message and started talking about this mad French girl she'd met in the club who'd told her she had nice breasts. Thank God, she always knows when to change the subject.

We made it back to the hotel with a minute to spare before my midnight curfew expired. I was really tired. All I could think about was getting to bed and going to sleep so I wouldn't have to think any more.

I went to get the key from the night receptionist but it seemed that Mia had come back early and was already in our room.

'I hope she's not asleep,' I whinged to Shona as we climbed up the stairs. 'If she starts screaming at me I'm going to cry.'

Our banging on the door could have woken up a coma victim but strangely enough it didn't rouse Mia from her slumbers. It wasn't hard to suss out her evil plan to make us sleep in the corridor because Shona had snatched Paul out of her nasty clutches. I slid down the wall so I was sitting on the floor.

'It's not fair,' I muttered. 'She could at least let *me* in. I mean, I'm not going out with Paul.'

'Oh cheers, Edie,' snapped Shona. 'Nice to know I can rely on you for a bit of female solidarity. Can you go and get the spare key from the receptionist?'

'Nope because there isn't one. She said, or I think she said, that Mia had gone and got the spare key because she'd locked the first one in the room by accident.'

'How convenient,' hissed Shona.

'Don't take it out on me,' I moaned. Being practically catatonic with tiredness never improves my temper. 'I'm as hacked-off as you are.'

'We'll have to find Martyn,' decided Shona. 'What room is he in?'

I gave a little shrug. 'How should I know?'

Shona actually screamed in frustration. God, she was such a drama queen sometimes. 'You could at least try and help.'

Paul suddenly stuck his head round the door opposite. 'I thought I could hear your voices.'

'Paul!' cried Shona, her face lighting up like she'd just had her batteries recharged. 'I didn't think you'd be back for ages.'

'We left straight after you.' He lowered his voice

and nodded in my direction. 'Dylan was in a funny mood.'

Shona leaned back against the wall and gave Paul a hopeful look.

'So are you going to invite us in or are we going to spend the night sleeping on the fire escape?'

Paul held the door open. 'After you, ladies.'

I didn't want to go through the door. I didn't want to see Dylan, not just because of all the kissing and the dragging away that had happened when I last saw him but also because I was worried that he might be wearing his pyjamas and I'd go off him or something.

I looked mournfully at Paul who was still holding the door open.

'What's the matter with you?' he asked in an amused voice.

I couldn't tell him that the last time I'd seen Dylan he'd had his tongue down my throat and his hand up my skirt so I whimpered and slunk into the room.

Dylan, thank God, wasn't in his pyjamas. He was still wearing his jeans and green T-shirt but he didn't look at all pleased to see us. He just nodded curtly at me and it was hard to believe that an hour before he'd been curled around me. I sat down on the edge of one of the beds and hoped that we could get the room situation sorted out. It should have been easy. Their room was just as big as ours but they had two double beds and a single.

'OK,' said Shona bossily. 'Edie can ring House-keeping for some extra bedding and we can have one of the double beds.'

'What, you and me?' laughed Paul.

'Yeah, you wish, sad boy,' snorted Shona. 'I mean me and Edie!'

'Hang on,' interrupted Simon. 'That means that two of us will have to share a double bed.'

'So?' said Shona and I in unison.

'Can't be done, I'm afraid,' said Paul. 'It just wouldn't be right.'

'Aw, are none of you very secure about your sexuality then?' Shona cooed. 'Look if it makes you feel better, neither Edie nor I think you're gay.'

Dylan was staring morosely out of the window, but at the mention of my name he turned around with an evil smile. It wasn't one of his evil I'm-going-to-ravish-you-in-a-second type of smiles. It was way more malicious than that.

'Or Shona and Paul could have one of the double beds, Simon can have the single and Edie and I could bunk up in the other double,' he announced with a not inconsiderable degree of satisfaction. 'What d'you reckon, Edie?'

There was an uncomfortable silence from the others. I could feel tears pricking against my eyelids.

How could he embarrass me like that? And why did I suddenly go to my happy place at the thought of smooshing together with him all night?

'I'm going to sleep in Nat and Trent's room. They've got two beds in there,' I mumbled. I peeled myself off the bed and had one hand on the doorknob when I heard Dylan say, 'Well, at least neither of them will lay a finger on you.'

'Precisely,' I snapped.

Dylan looked me up and down slowly and sneered. 'Don't flatter yourself, honey. Go and stay with your little gay friends, you're not ready to start playing with the big boys.'

'Dylan that was way out of order,' Shona hissed, just before I slapped him really hard around the face. His head jerked back as my hand made contact with his cheek. Dylan stood still and slowly rubbed his jaw where you could already see the imprint of my fingers.

'Touched a nerve, did I?' he enquired snidely.

'It doesn't matter if Nat and Trent are gay or straight, they're my friends and they treat me with way more respect than you ever have,' I yelled. 'You've been the one that's coming onto me. It hasn't been the other way round. You started every kiss that we've had.'

'And what's your point exactly?' asked Dylan, examining his fingernails like the whole conversation was too boring for words.

'Piss off. Piss off is my point,' I shouted because articulation was not my friend at that precise moment. 'Just leave me the hell alone.'

'Whatever,' said Dylan in a really bored-sounding voice. 'I thought you were different but I guess I was wrong.'

I wasn't even going to begin to work out what he meant by that. I was dimly aware of Shona calling to me but I was already out of the room and speeding down the corridor.

After knocking on the wrong door and waking up an irate French man and his wife, I finally found Nat and Trent's room and banged frantically on the chipboard.

'Let me in!' I called urgently, falling into the room as Nat opened the door. 'Can I sleep in here tonight?'

Then I burst into tears.

Nat and Trent were really good about it. They lent me a pair of pyjamas and while Nat gave me some of his chocolate stash, Trent wiped the smudged make-up off my face and sat with his arm round my shoulder, making soothing noises until I calmed down.

I sort of blurted out what Dylan had said about them but they didn't seem to mind.

'I've been called a lot worse than a "little gay",' joked Trent. 'Dylan's all right, Edie, he just gets a bit moody sometimes.'

Nat and Trent were probably the nicest, sweetest people I knew. And it had nothing to do with them being gay and/or sensitive, that was just the way they were.

'Don't tell me,' I said, holding up a limp hand in protest. 'You've known him since kindergarten.'

'Well, since the first year of the juniors,' laughed Trent. 'Look, Edie, me and Nat have had loads of grief from some of the lads at college because we're gay, but Dylan's always been cool with us. It's never made any difference to him.'

'He was probably just saying it to lash out at you,' added Nat.

'But why?' I wailed. 'He's all sweet and seductive when we're kissing and then he goes all grrrr and "my evil death ray will destroy Metropolis". You know what I mean?'

Whether they knew or not they both nodded sympathetically.

'He obviously has intimacy issues,' remarked Trent darkly.

'Yeah, like ninety-five per cent of the male population,' chimed in Nat. 'It's like a whole male imperative thing.'

'Well, that makes me feel a whole lot better,' I snarled. 'Thanks for clearing that up. It's really helped.'

'I can see your razor-like wit's back, you must be

feeling better,' Nat commented. 'Do you want the spare bed then?'

And the funny thing was that although I was sure that I wasn't going to sleep I dropped off before my head even crash-landed on the pillow.

Sunday

You know that split second when you wake up and you feel all right, and then you suddenly remember all the bad stuff that happened the night before? That's what happened to me the next morning. No wonder I was in a foul mood. I went back to our room to get washed and dressed just as Mia was leaving and the fact that she'd left the top off my toothpaste almost sent me through the roof. Muttering about her deep and frequent idiocy, I pulled on black cropped trousers and a black jumper. What was that line from that boring Russian play we'd been doing in English Lit? 'I'm wearing black because I'm in mourning for my life.' You said it, dead Russian guy.

I was just blow-drying my hair when there was a knock at the door. My heart leapt. God knows why, it wasn't as if Dylan was going to be standing there begging for my forgiveness. Anyway, it wasn't, it was Shona. She looked tired and pissed off.

'Hey,' she said cautiously. 'You all right?'

'Yeah,' I muttered. 'I'm not in a great mood or anything, but I'm OK. What happened after I left?'

Shona pulled a face. 'Dylan stormed out about two seconds after you did and didn't come back for ages and when he did he was drunk. Simon and Paul and me spent most of the night talking about how we should knock your heads together. So, I didn't get much sleep and I'm feeling very fragile,' she added warningly.

'None of this is my fault,' I snapped. 'Anyway, I've decided that I want nothing to do with Dylan from now on. He's just too much trouble and I don't need it.'

I expected Shona to be pleased. I mean, she was the one who told me that I had to stop mooning over Dylan but she just went, 'Hmmmm,' like she didn't really believe me and collapsed on the bed.

As I went down to breakfast I checked my phone and found I had three missed calls from Josh, even though I'd told him that receiving phone calls in France was expensive enough to bankrupt me. It put me in an even worse mood. I'd meant it when I'd told Shona that I'd have to break up with him but it didn't feel like a weight had gone from around my shoulders or anything. Instead it felt like once we got home I was going to have to go into hospital for major surgery. Just 'cause it's you that's doing the dumping doesn't mean that you get off scot-free in the heartache stakes.

OK, so I didn't want Josh as a boyfriend – but I still really liked him – and I didn't want to hurt him any more than I already had. I started to think of all the times that I'd been mean to him (and believe me there were loads) and how ungrateful I'd been when he'd given me the necklace for my birthday, not to mention snogging Dylan behind his back. I was, like, the worst girlfriend in the world.

Then something *really* horrible happened. As I walked into the breakfast room, all the conversation seemed to stop. Maybe I was being paranoid, but it seemed like everyone was whispering about me. Oh God, if they were, it was either about the clinch I'd got into with Dylan at the club or about me slapping him around the face or, even worse, both. Trouble, thy name is Dylan.

I concentrated on eating my toast and reading my book but I was aware of people casting furtive glances at me. I looked up, hoping to see Nat or Trent or Shona but they weren't around and then Dylan stumbled (that is the only word for it) through the doorway. Like me, he was dressed all in black and he looked about as bad as I felt. I mean, he never looks exactly flushed with good health but his face was ashen and he had huge dark circles under his eyes. I guess he had a killer hangover but, Dylan being Dylan, he managed to carry it off. He was really working that tortured artist thing.

I bent my head back over my book so he wouldn't realise that I'd been eating him up with my eyes. 'He's nothing to me, he's nothing to me,' I told myself over and over again. If I said it enough times I figured I'd start believing it.

The next time I looked up, to my horror Dylan was walking towards me with a cup and a pot of coffee. He couldn't be planning to sit with me, not after what had happened last night? He just couldn't . . .

. . . But he was and he did. After grunting a greeting, he collapsed into the chair opposite and sloshed some coffee into his cup.

'Want some?' he asked me.

I gave him my most frigid look. 'I beg your pardon,' I said icily.

'Would you like some coffee?' Dylan bit the words out.

'No, thank you.' It would have choked me.

We sat there in silence for quite some time. Dylan was clutching at his head as if he was in a great deal of pain, which pleased me immensely and I tried to read but I must have re-read the page in front of me at least five times. The words seemed to have stopped making sense. Even without looking at him, I knew that Dylan was watching me. I had to keep a tight rein on my body so it didn't do anything stupid like leap across the table and throw itself into his arms. *You're nothing to me, you're nothing to me.*

All of a sudden, Dylan planted one of his long-fingered hands across my page.

'Good book?'

'Do you mind? I'm trying to read,' I hissed at him.

'What's it about?' Dylan wanted to know. 'You don't seem to be getting very far with it, you've been reading the same page ever since I walked in.'

'I take it you don't have anything better to do with your time than watch me read,' I said.

'Not right now, no,' Dylan admitted.

'Look Dylan, please leave me alone,' I managed to say. 'We have nothing to talk about.'

Dylan removed his hand from the book and for a moment it seemed like he was about to reach out and touch my fingers, but he didn't.

'Well, I just wanted to say that I'm sorry. About last night,' he added.

'Which particular bit of last night?' I couldn't believe that I was being so hard. So in control. This was Dylan I was talking to. The boy who usually managed to reduce me to a pile of jelly.

Dylan leant back in his chair and gave me a searching look. 'I'm not apologising for kissing you. You wanted that as much as I did, but I'm sorry for the way I acted later.'

I glared at him. 'For what exactly? For being really offensive about Nat and Trent or that little comment, what was it? Something about me not being ready to play with the big boys, I think you said?'

He had the grace to look ashamed. 'I was completely out of order. I've said I'm sorry, Edie, what more do you want?'

I raised my eyebrows as high as they would go. He was unbelievable. 'How about an explanation? You kiss me, you make me believe that you actually care about me and then an hour later you're acting like a complete arsehole. You hurt my feelings.' It would have been better if I hadn't ended on a tiny sob.

I thought Dylan was going to ignore what I'd just said. For a little while he didn't say anything.

'I don't know, baby,' he said. 'I guess part of me did want to hurt you, or, like, wind you up. You just went off with Shona, you didn't even say goodbye.'

'What did you expect, Dylan?' I asked. 'Shona dragged me off. And anyway the only time you're ever nice to me is when you want to kiss me.'

'That's hardly fair,' he protested. 'I'm nice to you nearly all the time.'

'Yeah, but you always go weird on me, sooner or later. And I'm not going to forgive you for what you said about Nat and Trent. Not ever.'

Dylan was starting to look very haunted. I almost felt sorry for him. But, what the hell, he deserved it. This was all the stuff that I'd always wanted to tell him, but never had the guts. It was about bloody time he heard it.

'I've said I'm sorry, I can't do any more than that, Edie,' Dylan said, letting out an exasperated breath. 'I'll admit that I get jealous of the way you always run to Nat and Trent whenever you're down. We're meant to be friends, but you never tell me half of what's going on with you.'

'Yes I do!'

'You didn't tell me you were going out with Josh, did you?' Dylan said sourly. 'Not for ages.'

'Well, that's because you don't act like a friend. You spend most of your time being in a mood.'

'You can talk!' snorted Dylan. 'The only person I know who's more moody than me is you!'

'Yeah, well you make me moody,' I huffed. We were going round in circles. It was really hard to hate Dylan. I'd just decided that I was going to scrub him out of my life and then he decides to open up to me.

Dylan had his head in his hands by now. Maybe it was the hangover that was making him so, well, vulnerable.

'Are we cool then?' he was asking. 'We're friends again, right?'

I closed my heart and hung a big 'No Entry' sign on it for good measure. 'No, we're not cool,' I snapped, standing up and pushing my chair back. 'I don't want to be friends with you, I don't need friends that make me feel this shitty about myself.'

He groaned, like the whole situation was causing him great pain. 'What are you talking about now?'

I leant over, so our faces were inches apart. 'I've had enough of you,' I said, my voice going all wobbly. 'I can't take you snogging me and then treating me like dirt a few hours later. I just can't take your little mind games any more. You've already ruined the beginning of this trip for me, so just leave me to get on with the rest of it.'

Dylan looked completely shocked. What colour he'd had in his face slowly drained away.

'OK, I won't come near you, if you think that will make you happy,' he mumbled.

'I don't *think* it will make me happy,' I spat at him. 'I *know* it will make me happy.' And with that, I flounced out of the room.

But that was a lie. None of it made me happy. Half an hour later, as I dawdled down the street with the rest of the group, I was furious with myself. I couldn't believe half of the things I'd said to Dylan. I was so stupid. In fact, I was beyond stupid. Someone needed to invent a new word that meant stupid to the power of one million because that's what I was.

I could have taken advantage of hungover, understanding, apologetic Dylan to sort out our relationship, so we could be proper friends. The kind of friends who look out for each other and have a laugh and don't kiss. But, oh no, I had to jump in, firing away on all fronts, and basically tell Dylan never to speak to me again. That I didn't even want to share the same air space as him.

We were on our way to the Pompidou Centre, this modern art gallery complex. From the outside, it looked like a gigantic car battery, big and grey and covered in brightly-coloured tubes.

Shona and Paul weren't exactly all over each other, but they made it pretty clear that they just wanted to hang *à deux*. So Nat and Trent and me mooched round together. But even they were being majorly annoying; giving each other funny looks and muttering stuff that I couldn't quite hear.

When I'd given them a brief, censored account of what had happened with Dylan at breakfast, they weren't exactly supportive either.

'Christ, Edie, you were a bit brutal weren't you?' Nat had remarked. 'Is the word "kind" not in your dictionary?'

God, everyone seemed to think I was a stone-bitch but I wasn't. I was just, like, going through stuff. Anyway, I shuffled off on my own to buy some arty postcards, then went to find the others. At the back of the Pompidou Centre was a huge open-air piazza where every art boy in Western Europe seemed to have congregated. I've never seen so many pairs of skinny jeans, plaid flannel shirts and beanie hats gathered in one place. I was just starting to wonder if it was a government plot to get every art boy in existence herded together so they could mass-hypnotise them into being worthwhile members of society, when I felt someone watching me. All the little hairs on the back of my neck were tingling. I turned round slowly, expecting to find Dylan behind me but it was some guy I'd never seen before.

He was standing a little distance away from me and even though I was down with the whole world and boykind in particular, I couldn't help thinking that he was seriously cute. He had messy blond hair and a cool, second-hand suit on and when he saw me glance at him, he winked. I was seriously thinking about moving to Paris permanently. I mean, I had no luck with British boys but if Stéphane and Monsieur Le Cool Art Student over there were anything to go by, skinny pale girls with no breasts were obviously considered to be complete babes in France. Monsieur Le Cool Art Student was now mouthing something at me, when suddenly the others turned up.

'Bloody hell, Edie, we can't leave you on your own for more than a minute without you managing to pull,' teased Trent, looking at Monsieur Le Cool Art Student who was now making the international sign language for 'Would you like a drink?' at me.

'Him?' butted in Mia, knocking into me slightly. 'He's looking at me. It's obvious.'

I so wasn't going to rise to the bait.

'Nah, he's definitely into our Edie,' Nat decided.

'Oh yeah? Well watch this,' ordered Mia and off she sauntered in the direction of Monsieur Le Cool Art Student, swaying her hips like she had cockroaches in her pants.

'The Unstoppable Sex Machine strikes again,' laughed Trent. 'Oh Edie, looks like Mia's muscled in on your man.'

Mia was talking to Monsieur Le Cool Art Student in a really flirtatious way. She kept laughing, touching his arm and flicking her hair back as if she was auditioning for a part in a shampoo commercial. Within, like, the space of thirty seconds, her and Monsieur Le Cool Art Student were heading off arm-in-arm in the direction of a little café.

'Like I could really have a meaningful relationship with a bloke who wears studded wristbands in a completely non-ironic way.' I shrugged. 'She's welcome to him.'

Some of the art students decided to stay and eye up the talent, I mean sketch the interesting modern architecture of the Pompidou Centre, but I decided to go back to the hotel. The two-headed Shona and Paul smooching machine and Simon decided to come with me.

By now I felt like I had my own personal black storm-cloud situated firmly above my head. I stomped towards the Metro in silence.

'Hang on, Edie, I want to talk to you,' called Shona.

I turned round. 'Now what?!'

'You don't have to be like that,' said Shona, looking hurt. I swear, nothing helps a bad mood like spreading it around. 'I wanted to say that I was sorry, I should have been more sympathetic this morning when you were talking about Dylan. I mean, you were there for me when I was banging on about Paul and, you know . . .'

We went down the steps of the Metro station. 'What d'you mean by "you know"?' I asked her.

'Well maybe you wouldn't have been so . . . *fierce* with Dylan if I'd let you blow off some steam with me,' she finished uncomfortably.

'Don't take this the wrong way,' I told Shona as we headed towards our platform. 'But I don't want to talk about Dylan. He means nothing to me any more.'

'Oh come on!' said Shona incredulously. 'I know you're mad at him right now, but it'll blow over, it always does.'

'Not this time,' I said firmly.

'Look, I don't know exactly what you said to Dylan this morning 'cause he wouldn't tell me,' Shona confessed. 'But I do know it must have been something pretty devastating. I've never seen him this gutted. He thinks you hate him.'

It wasn't very nice but I couldn't help the little flame of triumph that suddenly started to burn. 'Well, he thinks right then,' I snapped.

Shona looked surprised, bewildered and then disgusted. 'I never knew you could be such a bitch,' she said quietly before turning away and walking back to Paul.

The train journey was hideous. Shona didn't speak to me, I didn't speak to her, which left poor Paul and Simon to plug the awkward gaps in the conversation.

Once we got back to the hotel, Shona stomped upstairs with a definite toss of her head. I was about to follow her and say I was sorry 'cause, bad mood or no bad mood, I hated arguing with her, when I realised that Madame La Réceptionniste was waving wildly at me. When I saw the telephone receiver in her hand, my first thought was that the 'rents had been in an accident. I rushed over to the desk and took the phone.

'Hello? Hello?'

'Edie, it's me. It's Josh, why haven't you returned any of my calls?'

'Oh hi, Josh.'

'I've been ringing your mobile but you never answered.'

'Well, yes, but my dad said it wasn't worth getting international roaming for five days and it costs a fortune to make calls back to the UK and I'm sorry but

I've been out all the time and there's been all this weird stuff going on, y'know.'

'You could have texted, at least. I was worried about you. I thought you'd let me know when you got there safely.'

'Josh, you sound like my mum! I'm sure if there'd been a three-lane pile-up on the autoroute you'd have heard about it on the news.'

'That's not funny. Look, I just wanted to wish you a happy birthday for tomorrow.'

'Cheers. I'll see you when I get back . . . I need to talk to you.'

'Don't go! Edie, I miss you so much. I think about you all the time, I'm counting the minutes till you get back. Are you missing me?'

'Look, Josh, you should, like, go out and stuff. You shouldn't be sat at home moping about me not being there.'

'I love you, you know that. I think you're great. You're just the best girlfriend in the world.'

'No, I'm not.'

'Yeah, you are.'

'NO, I'M NOT!'

'I think you are. I'm so lucky to be going out with you. Are you still there?'

'Josh?'

'What's up?'

'I was going to wait until I saw you but, but, there's

no easy way to say this, and it's nothing you've done. It's all my fault . . .'

'Oh God. You're going to dump me, aren't you?'

'I'm not dumping you. Well, yes I am. It's just I have, I mean I *had* feelings for someone else and I kissed him, or like he kissed me. It's not that I want to go out with him 'cause I don't, I hate him but I wouldn't have let him kiss me if things had been going really well with us, would I?'

'I don't believe it.'

'I'm so sorry. You're a really good person, Josh . . . I like you a lot but not in a boyfriend way.'

'Whatever.'

'You know, you could do so much . . .'

'Don't you dare say that I deserve someone better and don't say that you want to be friends. Save me the clichés.'

'Josh, I don't want to hurt you.'

'Well, too late, you already have.'

'Oh look, please don't be like this.'

'Christ, Edie, how do you want me to be? The only girl that I've ever felt anything for tells me that she's sorry but she's chucking me and, by the way, she's been seeing someone behind my back.'

'No! It wasn't like that, you've got it all wrong.'

'You said it, hon.'

Click.

* * *

'Well, that went well,' said Dylan from somewhere behind me.

I whirled round, still clutching the telephone receiver.

'Were you listening to my private conversation?'

Dylan looked unrepentant. 'I did try not to but you were being rather loud. Then it started getting really interesting and I thought, well, Edie already thinks I'm complete scum and she can't think any less of me, so I might as well stay and listen to the juicy bits.'

I put the receiver down, before I picked it up again and threw it violently at Dylan's head. 'I hate you!' I spat out childishly.

'So you keep saying.' Dylan gave me a smile that was completely without humour. 'I think that was just after you told him that we'd kissed. No, hang on, that you *let* me kiss you.'

'So?'

'So, you just stood there and *let* me kiss you?'

'What are you talking about?' I muttered. This conversation was starting to make me feel sick.

Dylan took a step towards me and I took a step back so I was pressed against the reception desk. Of course, Madame La Réceptionniste was nowhere to be seen. Which was a pity, 'cause Dylan looked like he was about to throttle me.

'I just want to get this straight in my head, Edie,' he said politely. Way too politely. 'I kissed you and you had nothing to do with it? You just stood there and suffered my attentions?'

'Well, not exactly . . .'

'You didn't kiss me back? And you didn't run your hands through my hair? Or wrap yourself around me? Or make those breathy little moans?'

Dylan was practically purring. Even though there were other people milling about, they all faded into the background so it was as if me and Dylan were completely alone.

'Shut up! Just shut up!' I all but screamed. 'Stop twisting my words. OK, we kissed. Are you happy now?'

'No,' said Dylan, sounding genuinely sad. 'I'm not happy at all. You're acting like I'm an evil, scheming piece of dirt.'

'I'm sorry,' I whispered, still clutching the edge of the desk like it was a life raft. 'I don't think that about you.'

'You know, we could go and see a film or something. It'd probably be in English with French sub-titles or it might be badly dubbed and then we could make up the dialogue ourselves . . .'

I couldn't help it. I started to cry. 'Don't Dylan, just don't,' I sobbed. 'I can't be friends with you any more. It's not working. We end up kissing and then it all goes wrong.'

Dylan started to wipe the tears from my face but I pulled away.

'What's wrong with being friends who kiss each other now and again?' he wanted to know. 'The kisses still mean something.'

'I can't,' I said, still crying. 'I just end up getting hurt.'

I really thought at that precise moment that Dylan was going to ask me out properly. Like, to be his girlfriend, but he didn't. He just muttered something I couldn't quite catch about 'not being able to do anything right', and walked away.

I spent the rest of the day moping. I moped in our room. I moped in the café down the street. I moped as I was getting ready to go out for dinner, and when I found myself sitting between Martyn and Tania, I moped some more.

When she wasn't scoffing huge quantities of mung beans and tofu, Tania watched every single mouthful I took. She'd convinced herself that I'd got a serious eating disorder. Obviously, no-one had told her about my addiction to chunky KitKats. There was still that really strange atmosphere hanging in the air. Almost as if everyone was in on this great joke except me. I was starting to wish that I'd never set foot on French soil. But at least one good thing happened . . .

I waited until Paul went to the toilets and then slid into the empty chair next to Shona, even though Dylan was sitting opposite. She gave me a look that was half reproachful, half contemptuous but I'd been expecting that. I didn't say anything, I just handed her a napkin that I'd prepared earlier. It had a little drawing of my face looking unhappy and a speech bubble with the words, 'I'm not a bitch, it's just the way I'm drawn.' It wasn't going to win me any awards for art but it did the trick. Shona looked at me and I looked at her while trying to stop my bottom lip from trembling and then she pulled me into her arms and gave me a hug. I rested my head on her shoulder.

'I'm sorry,' I muttered. 'I know I've been acting like an utter cow.'

'Oh, Edie, I'm sorry too,' Shona said. 'I have to stop sticking my nose into other people's business.'

'And I have to stop having hissy fits,' I promised but Shona just laughed.

'Why change the habit of a lifetime, kid?' she said.

Out of the corner of my eye, I could see Dylan pushing the food around his plate. He was glaring at his pizza like it had done him wrong.

'What's up, Edie?' Shona asked. 'You look done in.'

I rubbed my forehead. 'I've got a headache,' I told her. I wasn't lying. All the traumas of the day had caught up with me and were thumping around the inside of my skull. 'I think I'm going to go back to the hotel, I'm really tired.'

'Are you all right to go back on your own?'

I nodded. 'Yeah, Martyn's told me to get a taxi. I'll see you later, yeah?'

She squeezed my hand. 'I'll try not to wake you when I come in.'

As I got up and put my jacket on, everyone said goodbye to me but Dylan just sat there with his head bent, one of his fingers tracing the rim of his glass.

Monday

When I woke up the next day, I looked at the clock and it was eleven in the morning! I must have been bone tired. Then I was like, 'yay, it's my birthday!' until I realised I was on my own with just a couple of cards on the pillow next to me. One was from Mum and Dad (couriered over by Shona, no doubt) with a wad of euros in it and a message to get myself 'something nice'. The other one was from Shona, saying that she hoped that this year I'd get what I really wanted. The last three words were underlined about a million times. She'd also stuck a note on the envelope to tell me that I had to meet up with them at the Sacré-Coeur later.

I couldn't believe it. It was my birthday and I was all on my own. After I'd got dressed (I was definitely still in an all-black kinda mood), I dug out the Paris guide-book that Mum had insisted I bought and decided on a birthday whim to take a boat along the Seine (Paris's answer to the Manchester Ship Canal, if you ask me) to the Sacré-Coeur, which was basically a big white church. Yup, it was *that* exciting.

What was great was that the Sacré-Coeur (the Sacred Heart) was in Montmartre, which is this really cool part of Paris known as the artists' quarter. As far as I could tell, this means that lots of scruffy people with really good cheekbones sit around in cafés having deep philosophical discussions. Last night, Martyn had been boring me stupid, telling me stories about when he'd been a student and had spent two months living in Montmartre, growing a goatee and going to 'beat clubs'. I vowed to stay away from anyone with a goatee once I made it to Montmartre. I managed to find the boat place without too much trouble and even though it was quite cold, I sat on the deck. It might have been my birthday and I might have been a complete Betty No Mates, but there's not many girls from Manchester who get to travel down the Seine the day that they turn seventeen. Then, I couldn't help but remember what had happened the last time I'd been on a boat. As the wind whipped at my hair, it made me think about Dylan and how he'd sat on the ferry with me, stroking my face and staring deep into my eyes.

It seemed like I'd ruined everything that was good between me and Dylan. But he couldn't keep kissing me and expect everything to stay the same. He knew what kind of girl I was. The day that he'd come round to my house to sort things out, he'd told me that he needed a girl who was stronger than me and who wouldn't get hurt and how we should just be friends blah, blah, blah but our kisses had made that impossible. Dylan wanted to have his cake and eat it too and life just wasn't like that. At least, I didn't want my life to be like that.

When I got off the boat and looked at the Sacré-Coeur I suddenly decided that I wasn't going to waste my birthday clumping around a church. Sod it, I was going to have some quality time with me. Montmartre was all tiny cobbled streets and shabby cafés. Every time I turned a corner I seemed to fall over a street artist who wanted to draw my picture. They were all displaying really naff pencil drawings of supermodels as if to show how talented they were. Not even! When I wasn't telling them to go away, I was in severe danger of being brained by one of the thousands of jugglers who were chucking balls in the air. I hate jugglers. They all think they're all that just 'cause they can throw three orange beanbags at once. They should just get over themselves.

I could feel myself starting to get really stressed-out so I chose a swank-looking cake shop and gorged myself on the most deliciously gooey chocolate gateau and a hot chocolate while I wrote postcards to the 'rents and the grand'rents and some of my old friends from where we used to live. But it was hard to think of what to say:

Dear Mum and Dad

Having a wonderful time. Dylan's snogged my face off twice and now we're not speaking to each other. Everyone keeps talking about me and a huge hippy woman who doesn't possess a bra, thinks I'm anorexic. Please send chocolate.

Lots of love, Edie xxx

I don't think it would have gone down too well, so I settled for writing about the weather and how Hôtel Du Lac was situated in the middle of the red-light district, 'cause I knew Mum would have kittens when she read it!

Although I was trying to be all jolly and birthday-ish, at the back of my mind were all those unhappy thoughts about Dylan waiting to pounce. I ordered another hot chocolate and was just wondering whether I should try and find the others when it suddenly hit me. Shopping! I had a ton of euros to spend and a bit of serious retail therapy was just what I needed to chase all the darkness out of my head.

The guidebook stated that Montmartre was full of second-hand clothes shops, so I set out to buy myself the most beautiful, kick-ass, vintage dress that I could find.

Shopping is, like, the best way to make yourself happy. I bought an adorable, little green cardie with tiny glass beads embroidered along the hem and the cuffs for about a fiver, some Betty Boop hairslides, a notebook covered in Chinese silk and a box of beautiful French chocolates for the oldsters. I'd been walking round for ages and was just about to re-trace my steps back to the boat when I saw my dream dress.

It was the one thing on display in the window of a tiny, pink shop. Like, everything about the shop was pink. The walls were painted pink; there were pink plastic roses pinned to the ceiling; even the till was pink. But the slip dress in the window was mostly black. It seemed to be made of silk and was edged with pink broderie anglaise, including the tiny shoestring, shoulder straps. The girl behind the till smiled when I walked in and started squeaking in really bad French about The Dress in the window.

The shop girl took it off the mannequin and handed it to me, indicating a tiny curtained-off cubicle where I could go and change. I pulled off my jeans and jumper and carefully eased The Dress over my head. As I pulled The Dress down over my body, it transformed me. I stopped looking like a gawky, just-turned-seventeen-year-old and became elegant and sophisticated and well, sexy. Even my socks and trainers couldn't spoil the effect. 'J'aime la robe!' I told the pink girl as she stuck her head round the curtain and started 'Oooh la la-ing' at me.

It wasn't even that expensive, which just proved to

me that I was meant to have The Dress. I changed back into my clothes (which seemed so boring and ordinary after being in The Dress) and went to pay. When I told the pink girl it was my birthday she gave me a pink (what else?) plastic ring shaped like a rose, for free. I was so happy. But I was also very late. I decided that there wasn't time to get the boat back and headed for the Metro. Somehow, probably 'cause I was so excited about buying The Dress, I got on the wrong train and it was ages before I realised. I was determined not to let it ruin the day for me but by the time I raced up the stairs of Hôtel Du Lac, it was already past six o'clock.

'Edie! Where have you been?' Shona yelled at me as she opened the door of our room. 'I've been worried sick about you. I thought you'd been kidnapped or something.'

'I've been shopping,' I squealed. 'I didn't fancy the church and I was all depressed and I bought this fantastic dress.'

'Ooh, let's see!'

I took The Dress out of the pink carrier bag and held it out for Shona's approval.

She gave a long whistle. 'C'est très, très erm, groovy! Can I try it on?'

We were going to a French version of Pizza Hut for dinner but I still decided to get all dolled up. I mean, it was my birthday. But really I just wanted an excuse to wear The Dress. I was just zipping up my black, knee-high boots when I looked up to see that Shona had a really serious expression on her face.

My heart sank. She was going to talk to me about Dylan, I just knew it. And I'd almost managed to stop thinking about him. 'Look, Edie,' she began uncomfortably. 'I know it's your birthday but I haven't told anyone.'

'Er, OK. Why?'

She sat down on the edge of the bed. 'Well, it's just nobody's got any money and well, I didn't want them to be embarrassed about not getting you a present. I hope you don't mind.'

To be truthful, I did mind a little but I could also understand where Shona was coming from. Sort of.

'Don't be silly,' I said, giving her a smile. 'But you got me a present, right?'

Shona rolled her eyes at me. 'I wondered how long you'd last before you asked!' She rooted round on top of the wardrobe (I hadn't thought of looking there) and handed me a small parcel. 'Here you are, kid.'

I tore off the glittery paper excitedly and opened the tiny box I'd uncovered. Inside was a gorgeous silver necklace with tiny pink stones strung on it.

'Aw, it's beautiful,' I gasped. 'And it matches my dress. Thanks, Shona.'

I jumped up and gave her a hug.

'Happy birthday, Edie.'

* * *

I was determined to have a good time at dinner. But it was difficult. It really wasn't me being paranoid; everyone *was* being dead whispery. And Dylan looked like he was carrying the weight of the world (and the whole damn solar system too) on his shoulders.

He sat on the next table to me and I could see Simon trying to talk to him and getting ignored. I don't know how Dylan could think he was less moody than me. He could win Olympic medals for moodiness. I didn't flatter myself that Dylan was upset over what had happened between us – I think we've already established that he's king of the moody boys – but I wished that we could be friends. I was dying to tell him about the street artists and the jugglers (Dylan thinks that the only good juggler is a dead juggler), but it wasn't going to happen.

There was a hairy moment when Tania demanded to know why I hadn't made it to the Sacré-Coeur but I muttered something about how I'd wanted to take photos of normal Parisians and Martyn was so chuffed that one of his students had shown a bit of initiative that she'd had to let it go. Also Nat and Trent had slipped me a gift as I passed them on the way to the loo. The pack of feminist fridge magnets was just what I needed!

'I love the magnets,' I hissed at them as I sat down again. 'So, shall we go to a club after this?'

They exchanged a look, like they'd been doing for the last couple of days.

'Do I smell or something?' I demanded to know.

'What are you on about?' asked Nat.

'Everyone's being really odd,' I said darkly.

'You're the one who's being odd,' teased Trent. 'Anyway, I'm knackered, I don't think I can be arsed to go to a club. I know it's your birthday an' all . . . Ow!'

He looked at Nat and they both giggled.

'You two can be so immature,' I said crossly.

Shona and Paul wanted to go back to the hotel as well. I wasn't about to ask Dylan if he fancied clubbing it. I mean, I know we weren't friends any more but it wouldn't have killed him to wish me a happy birthday, as I said to Shona as we strolled arm in arm back to Hôtel Du Lac.

'Dylan's not very good about remembering people's birthdays,' she said lightly. 'I'm still waiting for my birthday present and that was, like, months ago.'

'He hates me,' I commented.

'He doesn't hate you Edie,' Shona contradicted me. 'You're just not his favourite person at the moment.'

'Same diff— The hotel's down there,' I added as she took a left.

'Short cut.'

'Are you sure, Shona?' I said worriedly. 'I don't think so.'

'Trust me,' she insisted.

We walked along the street for a bit and I realised that we were on our own.

'Shona, I think we're lost,' I hissed. 'The others have disappeared.'

'D'you reckon?' she said, sounding remarkably unbothered.

'What are we going to do?' I whined.

'You know, I think we should go to a club after all. Just the two of us. What do you think?' she suddenly announced.

I wasn't convinced. 'Not on our own. Not in the middle of the red-light district,' I said gloomily.

'Oh come on, it'll be a laugh,' Shona said, grinning. 'Look, let's try that place down there.' She pointed to a neon sign further along the street and started dragging me, protesting, towards it.

'I'm not sure, Shona. It could be full of weird people,' I said.

But Shona was already pulling me towards the entrance. 'Look, we'll just poke our heads round the door and if you don't like it we'll try somewhere else,' she promised.

'Well, it doesn't look very busy,' I pointed out as we entered the lobby. 'And it's dead quiet.'

I pulled open a door which I thought might lead to the main room of the club and then everything exploded around me. The lights suddenly blazed on, streamers were going off over my head and Nat and Trent and Paul and Simon were hugging me and shouting.

I turned to Shona who was laughing at me.

'Jesus, Edie, you can be so dopey sometimes. It's your surprise birthday party, you idiot!'

Monday, late

I was so relieved! Not only was I going to get a proper birthday but no-one hated me. All the whispering had been about the party.

'I can't believe you managed to keep it a secret from me,' I said to Shona as she led me to a table.

'I can't believe it was so easy,' she said, cackling. 'I've never realised how unaware of stuff you are. You were so busy angsting over you-know-who, that everything else just passed you by.'

'Is he here?' I couldn't help myself asking, though I didn't really want to know the answer.

'I don't think so. Do you want me to ask Paul?'

'No, it's all right,' I muttered. 'I can understand why he's ducked out.' I managed to smile at her. 'I'm going to have a good time, with or without him.'

Funnily enough, I did have an ace time. The DJ played lots of shouty, dancey music, Nat and Trent carried in a birthday cake with seventeen candles on it and Martyn let me have a couple of glasses of fizzy wine that he pretended was champagne. As if!

Maybe it was my beautiful new dress or the fact that everyone had made such an effort to plan a surprise party for me, but I felt like the girl with the most cake. Almost.

I think I danced with every single art boy at least twice and I was mucking about on the dancefloor with Nat and Trent when I looked up and thought I saw Dylan standing by the DJ booth. When I looked again, he'd gone. Then I saw him. He was standing slouched against the wall, frowning at me.

It was my birthday and I didn't want it to be like this between us.

I adjusted my resolve face and marched over.

'Hey,' I said.

He raised an eyebrow. 'Hey, yourself.'

I took a deep breath. 'Do you want to dance?'

Dylan shrugged. 'I don't do dancing.'

He wasn't going to make this easy for me but it was one of those moments when I knew that what I decided to do next would change the whole pattern of my life forever. I could either walk away and forget about Dylan or I could do what I did, which was grab his hand and pull him towards the dancefloor.

'Oh, leave me alone, Edie,' he groaned, but he didn't pull away.

'It's my birthday,' I pleaded. 'Do you hate me so much that you won't even dance with me?'

He shook his head. 'I don't hate you. You annoy the hell out of me sometimes but I don't hate you.'

That was as good as it was gonna get but then the

DJ started playing *Here Comes The Sun* by the Beatles and Dylan took my hands and we started dancing.

Well, I say dancing but mostly I just kept my feet moving and hoped that I was kind of in time with the music. But I figured, what the hell, I was wearing a magic dress and Dylan was holding my hands and the Beatles were singing, '*It's all right . . .*' and in that moment I knew that things were going to be OK.

The song seemed to finish as soon as it started but Dylan didn't let go of my hands.

'I think the club closes in a little while,' he said. 'Shall we get out of here?'

I thought about it for a fraction of a second before nodding.

'Wait for me by the door and I'll go and get your coat.' He let go of my hands and gave me a little push towards the exit. I stood there and watched Dylan hunt for my coat and have a word with Shona. She seemed to be giving him a hard time, but he didn't look too bothered. Then he started walking over to me and I stared at the floor like it was the most interesting floor I'd ever seen. The sight of Dylan loping across the dancefloor with his loose-limbed walk was doing flippy things to my stomach.

He held out my coat and helped me into it, just like the men do in those black-and-white films they always show on BBC2 on Sunday afternoons.

'You ready?' he asked but it wasn't a question, more like a statement.

'What about my stuff?'

'Shona will sort it out,' he said, grabbing my hand again before leading me through the door and up the stairs to the street.

'I don't think you've ever walked me home before,' I said as we walked along the road.

'Oh, I thought we'd find a café,' said Dylan casually. 'Y'know have a drink, or something. We need to talk, don't we?'

I hate it when people say that. It's the phrase that my mum always uses when she's about to lecture me about my bad attitude or lack of motivation: 'We need to talk.'

Dylan took my lack of response as a yes and was already pulling me across the street towards the same café that Shona and I had gone to a couple of nights before.

'D'you want a beer?' Dylan asked me, once we got inside.

I pulled a face. I hate the taste of beer. 'A cup of tea please,' I said. 'I'll go and find a table.'

I chose a table pushed far into the corner where it was dark so I wouldn't make a show of myself if I started crying and sat down with my back to the wall. Dylan was at the counter, pointing at the beer in the chiller cabinet and trying to mime the actions for a cup of tea. It was comforting that he didn't always get to be the cool one.

He walked to the table, rolling his eyes at me as if to say, 'I was a bit crap then, wasn't I?'

As he put the drinks on the table and sat down I noticed an envelope balanced on my saucer.

'What's this then?'

He smiled warily at me. 'You didn't think I'd forget your birthday, did you? Open it.'

I tore open the envelope and pulled out a card. It had a fluffy kitten chasing a bauble on the front of it. I gave him a look.

'It's meant to be ironic, OK?' he murmured.

I opened the card and a Polaroid fell on to the table-top.

Dylan picked it up and handed it to me. 'This is your birthday present. I was going to give it to you when we got back home.'

It was a picture of me! Dylan had taken a photo of me, reproduced the image twelve times, each time painting my hair and my eyelids and my mouth a different colour. It was like those famous Andy Warhol silkscreens of Marilyn Monroe.

'Wow!' I whispered. 'I don't know what to say. It's fantastic.'

'I figured you'd like it,' Dylan commented.

I opened the birthday card again to read the message inside. Dylan had written, 'To Edie, Happy

Birthday. I wish you everything that you'd wish for yourself. Dylan.' Cryptic much. There were no kisses after his name.

I took a sip of tea. Dylan was looking at me from under his lashes; it was a cool, considered look, as if he was weighing me up, trying to judge what kind of mood I was in. It made me feel very awkward. I started burbling on about what I'd been doing that day, the jugglers and the pink shop. I rattled on and on but I got no reaction from Dylan. Eventually I had to pause for breath.

'What are we going to do?' he said bluntly.

'About what?'

His lips twisted. 'About us,' he stated firmly. 'We can't go on like this, can we?'

I shook my head. 'I guess not. So, do you think we can be friends? Do you think we can, sort of, um, stop kissing?'

Dylan stared at me and for a moment I didn't think he was going to reply.

'No, I don't think so,' he said with a sigh.

'You don't think we can be friends any more?' I asked in a broken whisper. My right hand, which had been resting on the table, started shaking. Like, I had no control over what it was doing. Dylan reached out and gently covered my cold hand with one of his.

'No, I don't think we can stop the kisses,' he told

me. 'They're too good. I feel like my life is just periods of waiting before I get to kiss you again.'

I think, at that point, my heart missed a beat. And then I said it right away while I still had the guts to say it.

'I love you,' I choked out. 'I can't help it. And I know you'll come up with a million reasons why we can't go out with each other, but that's my one good reason why we should.'

I looked Dylan right in the eye and he looked straight back at me. It was impossible to suss out what was going through his head. He was stroking the underside of my wrist in an absent-minded way before he grabbed both of my hands and gave them a little shake.

'Listen to me Edie,' he said urgently. 'I think you're amazing. You're, like, the most alive person I know. Everyone else seems to move at half their natural speed compared to you. And when I'm with you, you make me realise things that I've never even thought about before. Like, when we were on the ferry and you were talking about the wind and the sea and stuff.'

'But I feel the same way when I'm with you,' I interrupted, but Dylan shook his head.

'No, let me say this,' he ordered. 'I can't get you out of my head. I just imagine what you're going to be like ten years from now and all the brilliant things you'll be doing and, like, how if you ever have kids how cool they'll be. And I think that if I went out with you, I'd make you lose all the things about you that are so special. You see the good in everything and all I can see is the bad stuff and the darkness. Do you understand what I'm saying?'

I nodded my head. I understood what he was saying, even if I didn't agree with it.

'But you're wrong, Dylan,' I insisted. 'Before I started being friends with you and Shona, I didn't have anything to say to anyone. I was shy and boring. And all the stuff that you've just said about me, that amazing stuff, you're the one who's inspired me to be like that. You've made me realise that I don't have to be frightened to tell people about what's inside my head.'

Dylan looked even more miserable once I'd spilled out my little speech.

'But there's other reasons why I won't go out with you,' he bit out. 'It's too much responsibility, I'd have to spend all my time being someone else because if I'm myself I'll just end up hurting you. And you're too young and I'm used to older girls . . .'

'Because you can sleep with them!' I snapped. 'That's what this is all about, isn't it? You want a girlfriend who'll have sex with you and you know I'm not ready for that.'

Dylan shifted uncomfortably in his seat. 'That's partly true,' he finally admitted.

'So, you think it's OK for us to be friends and for me to snog you and then what's going to happen when you meet one of these older girls? You still get to be friends with me but you stop kissing me and have sex with her instead. And that's not supposed to hurt me?' I finished with an angry intake of breath.

'I hadn't thought about it like that,' Dylan said. 'There doesn't seem to be an easy answer, does there? Whatever I do, it will end up being the wrong thing.'

'Not necessarily,' I protested, without actually thinking about where I was going with all this. 'Look, I'm not prepared to be second best. I'm giving you an ultimatum, we either start seeing each other properly or we stop being friends. I want everything or nothing.'

I think I shocked Dylan as much as I shocked myself. He took a long gulp of his beer and then looked at the ceiling as if he'd find the answer up there. It felt like the walls were closing in around me as I waited for him to respond. It could only have been a few seconds that passed, but they felt like hours.

Then Dylan scraped his chair back and stood up. This is it, I thought, he's going to walk out and we're not even going to be friends any more. I could feel this great, big sob welling up inside me but Dylan wasn't walking away, he was sitting down next to me and the next thing I knew, he was cupping the back of my head and kissing me really gently on the mouth, as if he was frightened that I'd break in half.

He started kissing a little path across my face until he reached my ear. 'OK, I'll go out with you,' he said softly.

I suppose when I'd thought about it, I always imagined that there'd be a loud clap of thunder and that lots of angels playing harps would suddenly descend from the heavens once Dylan finally said the words. Finally gave in and saw sense. Finally got beaten down by my tears and my tantrums and my utter rightness in the face of his utter wrongness. But, y'know, not so much.

I half-turned and hugged him and then he kissed me lightly on the lips again.

'Happy Birthday, Edie,' he drawled and he kissed me again. Greedy kisses, like he'd missed me.

Then we got kicked out of the café by the proprietor who was scandalised by our public display of affection. Dylan took hold of my hand and we ran down the street laughing.

As we neared the hotel, Dylan started kissing me again, his hands in my hair. I couldn't believe that I'd been stupid enough to think I could have walked away from Dylan and the feel of his mouth on mine. I pulled away.

'What made you make up your mind?' I wanted to know.

Dylan stroked a hand down the side of my face. 'I

couldn't walk away from you,' he said. 'And I s'pose I realised that we're practically going out anyway, so, y'know, we should make it official. Anyway,' he added with a wicked glint in his eye. 'It's not like I had to worry about the competition any more.'

'What competition?'

'Josh,' Dylan reminded me. 'I thought about how angry I was when you started going out with him. Like, how could he ever appreciate you like I do?'

I gave a little grimace. 'I'd forgotten about Josh,' I said ruefully.

Dylan smiled smugly. 'Good.'

When we got back to the hotel, we found Simon sprawled unconscious in one of the chairs in the lobby.

'Is he all right?' I asked one of the art boys who was sitting next to him.

He and Dylan laughed. 'Well, he won't be in the morning,' Dylan said. 'Once he passes out, it's impossible to wake him up, he's going to feel like crap tomorrow.'

'Up for some more drinking?' the art boy asked Dylan. 'Andy's having a party in his room. Y'know, last night an' all.'

I'd forgotten that we were going home tomorrow. Dylan looked at me and shook his head.

'Nah, Edie's tired.'

I was about to tell him that I wasn't that tired – I

couldn't have felt more awake if I'd tried – but Dylan shot me a warning look.

'Art student parties are horrible,' Dylan laughed as we began the trek up the stairs. 'Someone would've probably puked on your dress.'

When we got to my door, it was a bit awkward. I didn't know if Dylan wanted to come in or if he wanted to go to the party or what?

'Have you got your key?'

'Oh, it's a long story,' I sighed. 'Mia's got both keys but I think she'll let me in.'

I banged on the door. No reply. I banged a bit louder.

Dylan folded his arms and settled himself against the wall like he was in for a long wait. 'Maybe she's gone to the party.'

'Hmmm, maybe,' I agreed.

'So . . . D'you wanna come into my room?' he husked.

God, I'd forgotten about Dylan's sultry way with an arched eyebrow for at least half an hour. I looked at him and just about came undone.

'All right.'

He straightened up from the wall and walked across the corridor.

'You coming then?'

Dylan was holding the door open for me. The few steps towards the open door seemed to take forever, but then I was in his room.

'It's very tidy,' I commented brightly and tried to remember that it was just four walls and a floor and a ceiling. 'I thought boys were dead messy.' I couldn't think of anything else to say.

'I'm an art boy,' joked Dylan. 'I hate mess.'

'You're forgetting that I've seen the inside of your car,' I reminded him. 'It looks like a tramp died in it.'

'Are you going to sit down?' Dylan asked me. I was standing in the middle of the room, twitching because I felt so nervous. I perched on the end of the nearest bed and smiled uneasily.

'Relax, Edie,' Dylan smiled. 'Take your coat off, I'm not going to eat you.'

I shrugged my coat off and wriggled up the bed so I could rest a pillow behind my back.

Dylan came and sat next to me.

'Well, this is cosy,' he said.

I didn't really know what to say. There were a million thoughts racing through my head. Like, Dylan was my boyfriend now. And I was on my own in a hotel room with him and he was being dead . . . smoochy with me.

'Oh, don't go all shy on me,' he groaned.

'Well, stop looking at me like that.'

'Like what?' he murmured, giving me one of his most smouldering stares.

'Like that!'

Our eyes met and I knew that we were going to

start kissing in precisely three seconds . . . one, two, three.

Dylan's mouth came down hard on mine. One of his hands cupped my chin while the other crept round my waist, turning me towards him. He nipped at my bottom lip with his teeth before sliding his tongue into my mouth. It felt so right, I didn't want it to ever stop but my boots were really pinching me. I tickled Dylan under his arm.

'What?' he said, laughing softly.

'My boots are hurting,' I whispered. 'I have to take them off.'

When you're in the middle of a serious kissing thing, everything you say sounds really intimate, even mundane stuff about footwear.

I unzipped my boots and kicked them off and reached for Dylan again but this time I ended up lying flat on the bed with him half-lying on top of me. I could feel his ribs digging into me but I didn't mind, especially when he started nibbling on my neck and stroking along my collar-bone with his fingertips.

'We're just going to kiss, right,' I reminded him softly. I didn't want to kill the mood but I was worried that things might get out of hand unless I set some boundaries while I was still capable of rational thought.

'Don't worry,' rasped Dylan. 'There are thousands of things that I want to do that involve just kissing you.'

'I love kissing you,' I said dreamily.

'I love kissing you too,' said Dylan, smiling. 'And I love these little freckles on your shoulder. I think I'm going to kiss every one.'

It was true. Dylan could make kissing the most exciting activity in the world. He kissed my shoulders and then stroked all the hair back from my face, before planting little butterfly kisses on my forehead and my eyebrows and my eyelids before reaching my mouth again. And when he kissed my mouth, it wasn't like those kisses you tell your friends about where you joke about boys trying to slip you a bit of tongue; it was as if he was touching my soul.

Eventually we had to come up for air. It was getting cold and while Dylan went to get me a glass of water, I rubbed my arms and tried not to shiver. Magic dresses are all very well but they're not very warm. When he came back, Dylan climbed onto the bed and pulled the covers around us. He curled himself against my back, put his arms around me and kissed the back of my neck.

'Do you think Shona or Mia are back?' I asked.

Dylan groaned. 'Oh, don't go yet. I never get you to myself.' I could feel him laughing.

I reached behind and poked him. 'What are you laughing about?'

He kissed the back of my neck again. 'I don't know why I held out so long,' he whispered in my ear. 'I think you're going to be the most perfect girlfriend in the world.'

Hearing him call me his girlfriend made it suddenly seem real. Like, I'd achieved the impossible. After all these months and all the kisses that didn't lead anywhere and all the times we'd argued, I was in Dylan's arms and it was for keeps. Hopefully.

'Call me your girlfriend again,' I demanded.

'Edie's my girlfriend. My girlfriend's called Edie,' Dylan chanted, laughing again. 'See that girl over there with the really wicked eyebrows, that's my girlfriend, Edie.'

Dylan was running his fingers along my arm and it made me shiver in a way that had nothing to do with the cold and when he started gently biting my earlobe, I began to tremble.

'Calm down,' he said softly. 'I'm not going to seduce you or anything.'

'It's the anything I'm worried about,' I mumbled. 'Dylan? You don't mind about, like, me not wanting to, y'know, do it?'

Dylan paused mid-nibble. 'Well, I'd be lying if I said I didn't want to,' he confessed. 'But I want to make you happy and if you're not comfortable about having sex, then it's cool with me. Plus if you can't actually say it, then you're probably not ready to do it.'

'I'm so not,' I told him. 'Y'know, it's a really big thing. It's like the biggest thing in the world and there's all these things I don't know about you. And I haven't been round to your house and we haven't even been on a proper date and I'm not saying that once we do, I'll have sex with you, I'm just saying . . .'

'Shush,' breathed Dylan. 'It's all right. If you want to have sex some time in the future, that's fine with me and if you don't, that's fine with me too.'

Of course, I couldn't just let it drop. 'Are you sure?'

'Edie, it's been hard enough just getting together with you,' Dylan insisted. 'I'm not going to drop you just because you don't want to have sex with me. I don't think I could handle the trauma.'

I pinched his arm lightly. 'Huh! How can you say it was hard getting together with me when I had to force you to go out with me?' I demanded, but I put my hands over his hands, which were still clasped around my waist so he'd know that I wasn't mad at him.

I could feel that low rumble of laughter against my back again. 'I was just playing hard to get!'

'Oh, that's what it was,' I said. 'So have you slept with loads of girls?'

'Edie?'

'What?'

'Shut up and give me a kiss.'

We had another long bout of kissing before I got out of bed.

'Look, why don't you spend the night in here?' Dylan said. 'You could sleep in one of the other beds.'

'But what about Paul and Simon?' I pointed out.

'Simon will stay where he is until morning and for all you know Paul could be tucked up with Shona in your room,' Dylan protested.

'What with Mia in there too?' I said incredulously.

Dylan shrugged. 'She's probably crashed out at the party.'

'Under some willing art boy,' I said snidely, before I could stop myself.

Dylan just rolled his eyes as I put my coat on 'cause it was freezing, picked up my boots and headed for the door.

'Sweet dreams, girlfriend.'

One minute later, I was knocking on his door again. Dylan opened it, and raised his eyebrows at me.

'I thought you might be back,' he remarked.

'There's still no answer,' I explained. 'Can I sleep in here then?'

Dylan stretched, his black shirt rising up to show several inches of lean stomach. I looked away but he didn't seem to notice.

'Yeah, 'course you can,' he said.

I shrugged my coat off again and let it land on the floor while I hurriedly jumped back into the bed I'd just got out of.

'Jeez, Edie,' Dylan complained half seriously, picking up my coat and putting it on the door hook. 'What did your last slave die of?'

'Hard work!' I said. 'You tired?'

'Not really,' Dylan shook his head. 'Are you?'

'A little bit,' I admitted, snuggling under the covers again. Dylan lay down on the bed beside me but didn't make any effort to get under the blankets with me. He started undoing the little twisty knots I'd put my hair in earlier and combed the tangles out with his fingers.

I love having my hair stroked. It makes me feel like a little kid again. Dylan was talking to me but I didn't really pay any attention to what he was saying, I could feel my eyelids getting heavier and I rubbed my head against his hand.

'Did you have a good birthday?' Dylan suddenly asked.

'It was the best,' I replied sleepily. 'Weird but good.'

'Bit like you then,' he murmured. 'Weird but good.' He put his arms round me but I moaned in protest.

'Don't stop stroking my hair! I'm nearly asleep,' I said drowsily.

'Oh God, I can see you're going to be demanding,' was the last thing I heard Dylan say before I fell asleep.

Tuesday morning

I couldn't quite work out what woke me up. It might have been the weight of Dylan's arm curled against my waist, or just the fact that Dylan was lying next to me.

I opened one eye, he was still lying on top of the blankets, his mouth slightly open and his chest rising and falling as he took deep, even breaths.

A pale, bleached-out kind of sunlight was leaking through the gap in the curtains and when I craned my neck to look at the clock on Dylan's bedside table it was six o'clock. I burrowed deeper under the covers and was just about to go back to sleep when a terrible thought occurred to me. Well, actually several terrible thoughts occurred to me. I sat bolt upright in bed.

'OH MY GOD!' I shrieked.

Dylan woke up with a start, then gave another start when he realised that I was there.

'I must have fallen asleep,' he said sleepily, pointing out the obvious. 'I was going to crash on Simon's bed.'

'Never mind that,' I whimpered. 'We're meant to be leaving in an hour. To go home! Everyone will have sussed out that I didn't sleep in my room . . .' I tailed off and looked across the room. The other two beds were empty. Dylan followed my gaze and then slumped back on the pillow and groaned.

I staggered out of the bed and hunted for my boots. Even though I was in the middle of a potentially catastrophic emergency, I hoped that I didn't look too skanky. My dress was all crumpled and I was sure my hair was going in all directions.

Dylan padded over to the door, opened it and peered out cautiously.

'There doesn't seem to be anyone about,' he called softly over his shoulder. 'I think the coast is clear.'

I grabbed my coat off the hook and was just about to leave when Dylan pulled me back.

'What?' I enquired sleepily. I just couldn't get my brain into gear.

Dylan rested his hands on my shoulders. 'You're *really* not a morning person, are you?' he chuckled. 'Come here.'

I was going to protest that I hadn't cleaned my teeth, but then Dylan was giving me a good morning kiss and I stopped thinking.

'So you haven't got any regrets about last night?' I asked him eventually. I'd half suspected that Dylan might get all moody on me today but he was certainly acting like I was his girlfriend. He shook his head.

'Last night was great,' he said. 'What about you, you still OK with it all?'

I was just about to answer when I got the strangest feeling that we were being watched. I looked over Dylan's shoulder and standing at the open door of the room were Shona, Paul and Mia, their eyes literally out on stalks. Dylan had realised I'd stopped paying attention to him, but he had his back to the others.

'You still here, Eeds?' he wanted to know.

'We've got an audience,' I mouthed at him.

'Huh?' Then light dawned. He let go of me and turned round to face them. 'Oh, hi,' he said casually. 'All right?'

Nobody said anything for ages and then Paul grunted, 'Uh, yeah, I've got to get my stuff from your, I mean, our um, room.'

Dylan winked at me. 'I'll save you a seat on the coach or, like, vice versa.'

As I started chucking clothes into my suitcase, Mia and Shona simply stared at me. I was trying to be ultra casual but they were making me feel really uncomfortable.

'I s'pose I've got time to take a shower,' I burbled, trying to fill the silence. 'Might wake me up. My hair feels like it's crawling off my head.'

Mia couldn't bear it any longer. 'You spent the night with him!' she burst out. 'I can't believe it.'

I glared at her. 'I didn't have sex with him. Not that it's any of your business.'

Mia ignored me. 'I mean I heard Dylan say, "Last night was great",' she continued. 'I think it's really sad that you slept with Dylan when you know he doesn't want to go out with you.'

'I didn't have sex with him,' I repeated. 'I couldn't get in here last night, because you were either refusing to let me in or were passed out drunk at the party, so I crashed out on one of the spare beds in Dylan's room. And, for your information, I *am* going out with Dylan so you can piss off!'

My speech took the wind out of Mia's sails for precisely five seconds. 'I don't believe you,' she snapped. 'You're such a slag.' She grabbed her bags and flounced towards the door. 'I bet Dylan only said he'd go out with you to get you into bed,' was her parting shot before she slammed the door.

Shona folded her arms. 'So, before you disappear into the bathroom for five hours, are you going to tell me what really happened?'

I told Shona about what had happened in the café and how I couldn't get into our room when we got back.

'But I didn't crash out on a spare bed,' I admitted. 'I slept in Dylan's bed and he slept on the bed, if you know what I mean, like, on the covers.'

'Jesus!' shrieked Shona. 'She shoots, she scores.'

'Well, not exactly,' I said. 'But I do feel like I've climbed Mount Everest or something.'

'Well, I had my suspicions, I have to say,' Shona confessed. 'Especially when Dylan spent weeks working on your birthday present. Then you stopped speaking to each other and I thought, nah, never gonna happen, but when he turned up at the party last night, I just *knew*.'

'Hang on,' I cried. 'Two days ago, you were telling me that I wasn't his type.'

'Well, that's when I was still stuck on the "never

gonna happen" default,' Shona told me exasperatedly. 'You don't know what it's been like for me. I've had the two of you coming up to me and whining about the other one. You've been whinging about how Dylan just wanted to be friends and he's been sulking because you were going out with Josh . . . You don't know how close I came to murdering the pair of you!'

'Well, I suppose he has got a funny way of showing that he's into me,' I said with a frown. 'He's spent the whole trip acting like he just wanted to be friends. I had to give him an ultimatum in the end.'

'I wouldn't worry about it,' reckoned Shona. 'You know how dumb boys can be. I guess it was hard for Dylan to see what was right in front of him.'

'I don't know,' I muttered. 'I'm happy, don't get me wrong, but I feel like it could all go horribly downhill. I'm sure that Dylan's going to get all toxic again.'

'Oh, I don't think he'd do that,' Shona declared. 'Yeah, he's a creature of unrivalled moodiness, rivalled in fact only by your own unrivalled moodiness, but he seemed pretty loved-up this morning.'

'So, where did you get to last night when I was frantically knocking on the door?' I asked her.

'Oh, we went to Andy's room for a party. Mia got completely drunk and me and Paul had to put her to bed,' Shona explained with a look of disgust on her face. 'And then you hadn't come back and I was beginning to think that you'd chucked yourself into the Seine in a fit of despair but Paul managed to take my mind off my morbid thoughts.' She gave me a lecherous smile and a wink. 'Anyway, you've got five minutes before you need to be in the lobby with your luggage, so I guess you'd better take a raincheck on that shower.'

'As if,' I wailed, grabbing my towel and practically running into the bathroom.

Even though I broke all showering world records, I was still fifteen minutes late. The coach driver was just about to shut the boot when I ran down the hotel steps, dragging my bags with me.

'Sorry,' I huffed at Tania who was looking seriously cheesed off with me. So, what else was new?

'It's a pity that somebody didn't buy you a watch for your birthday,' she said grumpily. 'Honestly, Edie, I feel like I've spent the entire five days having to watch over you.'

Duh! That's your job, I thought.

'I don't know why I bother half the time,' she went on as she climbed up the coach steps.

'I don't know why you bother any of the time,' I muttered under my breath, as I followed her.

I stomped down the aisle of the coach to a couple of wolf-whistles and as I made my way to where Dylan was sitting, I heard one of the girls whisper to me, 'Nice one, Edie! Was he any good?'

By the time I reached the seat that Dylan had saved for me, I was bright red. I looked at Mia who was sitting in the seat behind, like butter wouldn't melt in her mouth.

'You bitch!' I hissed at her. 'Have you told everyone?'

She smirked at me. 'Yup!'

Dylan stood up and moved into the aisle, so he could put my shoulder bag in the overhead locker.

'You can sit by the window if you want,' he offered. 'What's up?'

'Nothing,' I snapped, glaring at Mia.

Shona, who was sitting in the seat in front with Paul, turned round. 'It's just Mia living up to her reputation,' she told Dylan with a pointed look. I pressed my hot face against the cold window as Dylan sat down next to me.

'Don't worry about Mia,' Dylan said sounding remarkably unconcerned. But then he would. If people think that a boy's scored with a girl, he gets treated like a player while everyone thinks that she's a slapper. It's so unfair.

'I'm not worried about Mia,' I said. 'I'm just annoyed with her. Y'know I wanted this to be perfect and she's ruining everything before we've even got started.'

Dylan pulled a face. 'Life isn't perfect, Edie,' he told me, squeezing my hand. 'But you just have to know when to pick the right battles and Mia really isn't worth it.'

'I heard that,' hissed Mia from behind us.

'And?' Dylan sounded utterly unrepentant.

'I don't remember you saying I wasn't worth it when you were seeing me,' she said nastily.

'Do you know something, Mia?' Dylan asked her.

'What?'

'You're really starting to bore me.'

The journey to Calais was really uneventful, apart from Mia kicking the back of my seat continuously for the first hour. Everyone was knackered after last night's two parties and having to get up at the crack of dawn, so mostly people slept.

I didn't know if Dylan was sleeping, but he had his eyes shut. His dark hair, which he usually pushed back from his face every five minutes was flopping onto his forehead. He'd slumped down in his seat so his bony knees, in their dark blue jeans, were almost touching the seat in front and his arms were crossed over his chest. He looked so remote.

I started to worry. Really worry. About my reputation being in ruins thanks to Mia. About how I didn't really know Dylan at all. Like, I knew that he makes funny little snuffly noises when he sleeps but I didn't even know if he had any brothers or sisters. But what I really worried about was whether I'd forced Dylan into going out with me when he hadn't really wanted to. And, like, if we were dating did that mean that we'd only hang out as a couple, instead of being mates as well? I didn't want to be Dylan's girlfriend if it meant that I had to stop being his friend. By the time we reached Calais, I'd practically convinced myself that Dylan and I were going to split up before the end of the day. I was in the grip of a major depression. As the coach rolled into the ferry's bowels and came to a stop, Dylan opened his eyes.

'I needed that,' he yawned. 'I was so tired.' He stood up and stretched, ignoring complaints that he was blocking the aisle. 'I'm starving,' he announced. 'Are you lot coming?'

Shona and Paul murmured agreement and followed Dylan off the coach. I leant back against the window and then catching the annoyed look in Tania's eyes as she stood by the driver's seat, I slid out of the seat and trudged towards the exit.

'I wouldn't worry about Dylan if I were you, Edie,' Tania said to me with a smile, as we walked up the steps that led to the saloon. 'I think you've managed to find yourself a good one there.'

'How did you know?' I gasped.

'Oh, I was young once,' said Tania dramatically, in that patronising way that old people do. 'Seriously, Edie, I think Dylan, despite his cool exterior, has got a good heart. He'll look after you and, Lord knows, you need somebody to!'

'No, I don't,' I said mock-sulkily. Then a really hideous thought popped into my head. 'So, Tania, did you have a Dylan-like boyfriend when you were my age and please don't say it was Martyn?!'

'Ah, that would be telling,' she teased and I felt a bit guilty for thinking such mean thoughts about her, though I still reckoned that she could do with a well-fitting support bra. 'Now, get out of here and try not to fall overboard or anything.'

It's funny how people that you don't really know, or even like particularly, can tap into what you're thinking. My little chat with Tania had made me feel a bit better. Maybe I was just worrying about nothing. I was going to find Dylan and the others but I passed a snack bar and I got side-tracked. After all they were selling chocolate, proper Cadbury's chocolate, and it'd been five days since I'd had a bar of Dairy Milk . . .

I unwrapped my second bar and popped a chunk in my mouth. I'd had a quick look for the others but I couldn't find them and the sight of people being sick (it was another rough crossing) was starting to put me off my choccy, so I'd decided to find a seat on the open deck. Last time I'd sat up here I never thought that I'd be going home as Dylan's girlfriend. Mind you, I didn't feel like Dylan's girlfriend, I still felt like me; Edie Wheeler, who talked too much or not at all, had snogged four boys in her entire life and had £517 in her Post Office savings account.

'Hey!' I looked up to see Dylan standing in front of me.

'Hey yourself,' I replied.

'You look like you're deep in thought,' he commented, sitting down on the bench next to me. 'What were you thinking about?'

'How much money I've got in my Post Office account,' I said vaguely. 'Do you want some chocolate?'

I handed him my started-on bar and watched as he broke off a couple of chunks.

'Dylan?'

'Hmmmm?'

'Do you think we can still be friends even though we're going out with each other?' I asked him.

'Why? Don't you?' he said cautiously, angling a 'what is she on?' look at me.

'I don't know,' I replied. 'I hope so. We'll still do stuff together like go and see bands won't we? And go to the cinema and hang out with Shona? It won't change anything, will it?'

Dylan lifted one of my hands to his lips and kissed my fingers. 'Look, things have to change,' he said. 'But it doesn't mean they'll have to change for the worse. It's like I said last night, I think we were going out with each other all the time and we never even realised it. We've just made it official.'

'But we're more than just friends who kiss each other?' I asked him hesitantly. 'And I don't just want to be your girlfriend either.'

'But you're not just my girlfriend,' protested Dylan. 'Hey, you're my Edie! You could never be anything else. That's why I'm so into you.'

'Yeah?'

'Yeah.'

He rubbed his knuckles against my cheek and grinned.

'I wanted to kiss you so badly when we were going to France on the ferry. You know, when I stroked your face,' he confessed. 'Didn't you realise?'

'Nah!' I told him, my heart suddenly feeling so light that it could have been lifted away by the wind. 'I just thought you were admiring my delicate bone structure.'

I smiled at Dylan and he smiled back at me. Our eyes met and I leaned forward to brush my lips against his. Dylan tasted of chocolate and coffee. Just along the horizon, the distant white cliffs of Dover came into view and I wondered if things could ever be the same again.

A NOTE FROM THE AUTHOR

I started writing *Diary of a Crush* fourteen years ago.

At the time I was Entertainment Editor on *J17,* a teen mag for teenage girls with plenty of attitude and a fondness for indie boys.

Every month I would write an emotional feature about boys or relationships or snogging (usually a combination of all three), until I could take it no longer and in a features meeting pitched writing a fictional account of a relationship: from crush to kiss to going steady, just because I was so tired of dispensing advice on how to make spoddy boys who probably weren't worthy of our readers fall madly in love with them.

My editor, Ally Oliver, greenlighted it; probably because I was clutching my hair and saying, 'I don't have it in me to write another snogging feature.' So off I went back to my desk and began to write the 1800 words that had been allocated to the piece.

I remember sitting there thinking about my days at college where I studied for my A-levels after being asked to leave the really strict girls' school where I'd done my GCSEs.

Going to college was when I really blossomed. I found a sense of independence, new friends and a love for the nineteen-year-old boys studying for their Foundation Art diploma. It was from this experience that Edie, a shy sixteen year old starting college, and Dylan, the tousle-haired art boy who catches her eye and her heart, were formed.

I'd only written for magazines and had no idea what I was doing. All I knew was that I was having huge amounts of fun (not to mention wish fulfilment) and *Diary of a Crush* was born.

But a couple of days later when Ally asked me how I was getting on, the news wasn't good. 'I've written 4000 words and they haven't even snogged yet,' I wailed.

Ally agreed to run *Diary of a Crush* over a few issues and so began a serial that lasted for more than three years. The *J17* readers completely embraced Edie, no matter how whiny she got, and her motley collection of friends. It was a lovely way to become an author.

What are gathered in these books are the monthly columns, plus the novellas I would write that were given away free with *J17* each summer (originally called *French Kiss, Losing It* and *American Dream*).

The bulk of the material here was written as monthly columns, so I would bang out 1200 words in an afternoon, then go to the subs and art departments and dare them to cut a single word. I took a week off each time I wrote a novella.

Before this, I'd never written fiction. Never been on a course or even read a book for budding novel writers. Instead, I learned on the job as I wrote *Diary of a Crush* and so I think Edie grows as a person as I grew as a writer.

The columns were originally tweaked to be turned into novels and with each subsequent edition I've made changes to some of the popular culture references, because mooning over Leonardo DiCaprio and, er, Blazin' Squad is not really an option these days. They were also originally written in the days before teenagers had mobile phones and long, long, long before Facebook or BlackBerry Messenger were invented.

I've also learned a lot more about book writing since then and there were some unforgivably bad sentence structure and syntax crimes going on that I've corrected. I couldn't have lived with myself if I'd let them slip through!

So while the trilogy hasn't been rewritten, I've given it a nip and a tuck and a general tidy up for maximum reading pleasure. I hope I kept to the spirit in which I originally wrote *Diary of a Crush* and I hope you enjoy reading about Edie and Dylan as much as I loved telling their story.

Sarra Manning, London, 2013.

Turn the page for a sneak peek at the next instalment from Edie's journal:

KISS AND MAKE UP

Edie's Journal
Manchester

8th April

I have this photograph of me and Dylan tucked into my diary. We're standing on the deck of the ferry on our way back from France in a force-ten gale, so his tufty dark brown hair is even more dishevelled than usual and that tender smile of his is diffusing the sharp lines of his face. Dylan's got his arm around my shoulders and he's squinting down at me and smiling fondly like I'm the greatest thing in the world. Even greater than our recent discovery that chopping up chocolate chip cookies and scooping them into vanilla ice cream will give you twice the sugar rush you normally get from eating them straight.

He certainly looks happy to be my boyfriend.

But over the last week I've made the startling discovery that having a boyfriend is nothing like I imagined. No. Scratch that. Having Dylan as a boyfriend is *exactly* how I imagined it. Or thought it might be in my worst nightmares.

All that stuff he came out with on the boat about how being boyfriend and girlfriend was going to be like we were before but even better? And we'd hang out with each other like we did before but there'd be all this amazing kissing and touching and, I don't know, boyfriendly behaviour? Well, not so much.

Because now that Dylan's my boyfriend, I have to handle his weirdness head-on. His weirdness has, like, rules. Not that he's given me a written list but if he did, it would go something like this:

1. Don't ever come round to my house. Ever.
2. Don't hold hands with me in public.
3. Kissing and touching and boyfriendly behaviour should be restricted to dark corners.
4. Pet names are strictly prohibited.
5. Don't expect me to call when I say I will or be on time for anything or come round for Sunday lunch with your parents.

Some of it is good. A lot of it is good. And my kissing technique has drastically improved with all the extra practice I'm getting but Dylan was way more affectionate when we were bickering mates.

9th April
I was sitting by the piddly college fountain with Shona when Dylan sauntered over to us.

'God, Edie,' Shona muttered when she caught sight of Dylan, 'you can't be planning to go off and make out *again*. You look like you've had collagen lip implants as it is.'

'Shut up,' I said plaintively. 'You make me feel like I'm just a big kiss slut.'

She arched an eyebrow. 'Oh, I must be getting you confused with someone else then.'

Then Dylan was there. 'Which hand?' he drawled, putting his arms behind his back. My heart leapt. Had he bought me a present?

'The left?'

Dylan gave me a huge, sunshiney grin. 'That was the right answer,' he said, swinging a key in front of my eyes.

'What's that?' I asked, though it was pretty obvious what it was, but I felt like I needed some clarification.

'It's the key to the darkroom. You coming?'

'Who said romance was dead?' I heard Shona hiss to no-one in particular as I jumped off the wall and followed Dylan in the direction of the art block.

I had been planning to tell Dylan a few truths, I really had, but once we got into the darkroom he immediately reached for me and I kind of forgot. Dylan had me wedged against the enlarger so I couldn't move but I didn't want to. I felt sort of boneless and lethargic like Pudding does when she's all sleepy and lying in the sun. Dylan's tongue was causing havoc everywhere it went when we were suddenly interrupted by the door banging open.

'Sod off,' snarled Dylan, not bothering to turn round, which was a pretty stupid thing to do. Or at least that's what Martyn, our Photography tutor, said when he proceeded to give us a major, major bollocking. With, like, knobs on. No pun intended.

Martyn frogmarched me to my personal tutor who sent me home for the rest of the afternoon. Which actually is my kind of punishment.

As I stood outside the college gates applying some Vaseline to my lips, which seem to be permanently desensitised from over-use these days, Dylan caught up with me.

'Soooo, are we going back to yours?' he purred.

'No! I was *this* close to being sent home with a note,' I snapped. 'You know my parents don't trust us to be alone.'

It's true. They don't seem overjoyed about me dating Dylan and he's forbidden from my room unless the door's open. It hasn't occurred to them that we could get up to all sorts of inappropriate touching in plenty of other venues but I'm not going to be the one to shatter their illusions.

'Oh, c'mon Edie,' he said, nudging me. 'I don't want to go home and Martyn told me to get out of his sight for the rest of the day.'

'Well, OK, then,' I conceded. 'I need to talk to you anyway.'

'That sounds ominous,' Dylan said out of the side of his mouth but then we spent the rest of the walk to my house in silence, which hacked me off.

It was like Dylan had forgotten how to speak to me.

'What the hell is your problem?' I blurted out the minute we got through the front door. 'Why aren't you talking to me?'

'I am,' he protested, following me up the stairs. 'You're the one who's not talking to me.'

'You're treating me like a . . . a . . . a kiss slut!' I said furiously.

Dylan snorted. 'Like, you don't treat me that way too.'

Then he sat down next to me on the bed and put an arm round my shoulders. 'Look, Eeds, this is a bit weird for both of us. So, what do you want to talk about then?'

I shrugged. 'Stuff. Like, y'know, stuff about each other. You never tell me what's going on with you.'

'The only thing going on with me is you,' Dylan snarked. 'There's nothing else to tell you about.'

If there was nothing else to talk about there was only one thing else to do: investigate each other's mouths with our tongues.

Two minutes later we were rolling about on my bed.

I think it was when we landed on the floor with a loud thud that my mum realised that the house wasn't empty. She came charging up the stairs and banished Dylan from the house forever for daring to lay his evil boy hands on her innocent, virginal daughter. It was all I could do to stop her from grounding me.

10th April

I didn't speak to Dylan today. I think the credit had run out on his phone. Which led to the revelation that I didn't have Dylan's home number. He always, always calls me. And that's weird. It's very weird. It's a whole world of weird. I've known Dylan for more than six months now. Been on intimate terms with his mouth for a little less time than that so you'd think I'd have his home phone number. I could have done the whole telephone directory thing but instead I went round to Shona's.

'So, are you going to have a go at me for not telling you about Dylan's dysfunctional family?' she wanted to know, a tad belligerently, when I asked her for his number.

I was like, woah!, but reined it back in. 'Look, I wouldn't expect you to betray Dylan's confidence,' I said sweetly. 'You're his oldest mate.' Which was actually her cue to explain what the hell she meant by her strange and cryptic remark about Dylan's family. His surname was strange, Kowalski (I think it's Polish or Czech or even Ukrainian or something), and I allowed myself a small daydream that Dylan's parents were dissidents from the former Eastern bloc and had come over to England to start a new life with their little baby Dylan away from the harsh totalitarian regime and the jackboot of Communist oppression, but I think that was heavily influenced by the module I was studying in History.

I came back from a vision of Dylan's very young, very beautiful mother shielding a baby Dylan away from a granite-faced Communist soldier to find Shona looking at me with an exasperated expression on her face. 'Did you enjoy the little trip you just took with the fairies?'

'Dylan hasn't said anything about having a dysfunctional family,' I said grumpily. 'In fact, he hasn't even admitted to having a family. I was beginning to think he was hatched in an art boy factory.'

Shona fiddled nervously with some of the piles of junk on top of her bedside cabinet. 'Sorry,' she muttered. 'Sometimes it's hard being stuck in the middle of you two.'

Then Shona started telling me about the eye-raising stuff (can I just say, ewwwww?) she was getting up to with Paul and how she reckoned Mia was behind these weird phone calls she was getting and I forgot about ringing Dylan.

By the time I got home, it was really late and The Mothership was fuming. So, like, what else is new? She and Dad were heading off to the grandparents in Brighton for a long weekend (thank the sweet baby Jesus) and they were convinced I had Dylan stashed down the road somewhere and was just waiting for them to leave so he could enter the house and violate me on the new IKEA rug. She said as much. When your mother doesn't want to have the sex talk with you any more but instead wants to talk to you about the possibility that you might have sex on her soft furnishings, it's a watershed moment in any girl's life. I know I'll remember it fondly for many years to come.

Anyway after much foot-stamping and gagging noises, which I've found work much better than rational debate, I managed to persuade them that I hadn't seen Dylan all day and they left. Then they came back to harangue me with instructions about the boiler and not forgetting to give Pudding her worming tablets. Then they left again. Time for some fish fingers and Mum's *Downton Abbey* box-set, I think.

10th April (later)

Oh God, Dylan's on his way round. I wasn't going to let him but when he heard that the 'rents were off the premises for forty-eight hours there was no stopping him. He didn't exactly ask if he could stay over but then it's 10.30 pm now . . .

Oh, hell, that's him at the door now . . .

**Because we like to spoil you,
turn the page for an extract from:**

ADORKABLE

SARRA MANNING

ADORKABLE

LOVE, HATE
WHATEVER

1

'We need to talk,' Michael Lee told me firmly when I stepped out of the makeshift changing room at the St Jude's jumble sale, which was actually four curtained rails arranged in a square, to have a good preen in front of a clouded mirror.

I didn't say anything. I just stared back at his reflection, because he was Michael Lee. MICHAEL LEE!

Oh, Michael Lee. Where to begin? Boys wanted to be him. Girls wanted him. He was star of school, stage and playing field. Enough brains to fit in with the geeks, captain of the football team so all the sporty types bowed down before him, and his faux-hawk and carefully scuffed Converses also pulled in the indie crowd. If that wasn't enough, his dad was Chinese so he had an exotic Eurasian thing going on; there was even an ode to his cheekbones on the wall of the second-floor girls' loos at school.

He might have been all that and a bag of Hula Hoops but, as far as I was concerned, if you were one of those popular types who got on with absolutely everyone then you couldn't have much of an edge. To be all things to all people, Michael Lee had to be the least interesting person in our school. That took some doing because our school was bursting at the seams with mediocrity.

So I couldn't imagine why Michael Lee was standing there in front of me insisting that we needed to have a chat, chin tilted so I had a great view of his poetry-inspiring cheekbones. I could also see right up his nostrils because he was freakishly tall.

'Go away,' I said in a bored voice, wafting my hand languidly in the direction of the other side of the church hall. 'Because I can guarantee that you have nothing to say that I'd want to hear.'

It would have sent most people scuttling back from whence they came but Michael Lee just gave me this look as if I was all hot air and bluster, then he dared to put his hand on my shoulder so he could turn my stiff, cringing body round. 'Look,' he said, his breath hitting my face, which made me flinch even more. 'What's wrong with that picture?'

I couldn't concentrate on anything other than Michael Lee having his football-playing, prize-essay-writing hot fingers on my clavicle. It was just wrong. Beyond wrong. It was a whole other world of wrong. I screwed my eyes tightly shut in protest and when I opened them again, I was looking at Barney, who I'd left in charge of my stall, against my better judgement, talking to a girl.

Not just any girl but Scarlett Thomas, who happened to be Michael Lee's girlfriend. Not that I held that against her. What I held against her was that she was vapid and had a really annoying voice, which was breathy and babyish and had exactly the same effect on me as someone crunching ice cubes. Scarlett also had long blonde hair, which she spent hours combing, spritzing, primping and tossing so if you stood behind her in the lunch queue there was a good chance you'd get a mouthful of hair.

She was tossing her hair back now as she spoke to Barney and, yes, she was grinning a vacant grin and Barney was smiling and ducking his head, the way he did when he was embarrassed. It wasn't a picture that made my heart sing, but then again . . .

'There's nothing wrong with that picture,' I told Michael Lee crisply. 'It's just your girlfriend talking to my boyfriend—'

'But it's not the talking—'

'About quadratic equations or one of the many other things Scarlett doesn't understand, which made her fail her Maths GCSE and have to retake it.' I gave Michael a flinty-eyed look. 'That's why Ms Clements asked Barney to tutor Scarlett. Didn't she mention it?'

'She did mention it and it's not them talking to each other that's wrong, it's how they're not *really* talking at all. They're just standing there and gazing at each other,' he pointed out.

'You're being ridiculous,' I said, even as I surreptitiously glanced back to where Barney and Scarlett were indeed gazing at each other. It was obvious they were staring at each other because they'd run out of things to say and it was awkward, nervous gazing, because they had absolutely nothing in common. 'There is *nada*, nowt, not one thing going on. Well, apart from the fact that you and Scarlett are slumming it at a jumble sale,' I added, turning my attention back to Michael Lee. 'Right, now that we've cleared that up, feel free to go about your business.'

Michael opened his mouth like he had something more to say about the utter non-event of Barney and Scarlett gurning at each other. Then shut it again. I waited for him to leave so I could go about *my* business, but he suddenly moved closer to me.

'There is something going on between them,' he said, bending his head. His breath ghosted against my cheek again. I wanted to bat it away with an irritated gesture. He straightened up. 'And nice dress, by the way.'

I could tell he didn't mean it from the almost-smirk on his face, which made me wonder if Michael Lee might actually have some hidden depths buried way below the surface of his bland exterior.

I sniffed loudly and contemptuously, which made the quirk of his lips blossom into a full-blown smirk before he strode away.

'Jeane, my love, don't take this the wrong way, but he was being sarcastic. That dress doesn't look at all nice,' said a pained voice to my left and I looked over at Marion and Betty, two volunteers from the St Jude's social committee who manned the cake stall and policed the changing room. One of their stern looks would scare off even the most determined perv. I didn't doubt that they'd pelt peeping toms with rock buns if the stern looks failed.

'I know he was being sarcastic but he was also being very mistaken because this dress is made from all kinds of awesome,' I said, stepping back so I could get my preen on, though my heart wasn't really in it now.

The dress was black and I didn't normally do black because why would anyone want to wear black when there were so many fabulous colours in the world? People with no imagination and Goths who hadn't got the memo that the nineties were over, that's who. But it wasn't just black; it had these horizontal patterns all over it – yellow, green, orange, blue, red, purple and pink squiggly lines that made my eyeballs itch – and it fitted so well that it could have been made just for me, which didn't happen often because I have a very odd body. I'm small, like five feet nothing, and compact so I can fit into children's sizes, but I'm sturdy with it. My grandfather used to say that I reminded him of a pit pony – when he wasn't telling me little girls should be seen and not heard.

Anyway, yes. I'm sturdy, stocky even. Like, my legs are really muscly because I cycle a lot and I'm kind of solid everywhere else. If it wasn't for the iron-grey hair (it was meant to be white but my friend Ben had only been training as a hairdresser for two weeks and something went badly wrong) and the bright red lipstick I always wore, I could have passed for a chubby twelve-year-old boy. But this dress had enough nips and tucks and darts and horizontal lines that at least it looked as if I had some kind of shape because me and puberty hadn't got on very well. Instead of womanly curves, it had left me with a general lumpiness.

'You'd look so pretty if you wore a nice dress instead of all this nasty jumble sale stuff. You don't know where it's been,' Betty lamented. 'My granddaughter's got lots of clothes she doesn't wear any more. I could sort you out some things.'

'No, thanks,' I said firmly. 'I love the nasty jumble sale stuff.'

'But some of my granddaughter's old clothes are from Topshop.'

It was very hard to restrain myself, but I didn't immediately launch into a rant about the evils of buying clothes from high street chains, which peddled the same five looks each season so everyone had to dress just like everyone else in clothes that were sewn together by children in Third World sweatshops who were paid in cups of maize.

'Really, Betty, I like dressing in clothes that other people don't want any more. It's not the clothes' fault that they've gone out of fashion,' I insisted. 'Anyway, it's better to reuse than recycle.'

Five minutes later, the dress was mine, and I was back in my own lilac-tweed, old-lady skirt and mustard-coloured jumper and heading to my stall where Barney was leafing through a stack of yellowing comics. Thankfully, Scarlett and Michael Lee were nowhere to be seen.

'I got you cake,' I announced. At the sound of my voice, Barney's head shot up and his milk-white complexion took on a rosy hue. I'd never known a boy who blushed as much as Barney did. In fact, I hadn't even been certain that boys *could* blush, until I met Barney.

He was blushing now for no good reason, unless ... No, I wasn't going to waste my precious time on Michael Lee's crackpot theories, except ...

'So, Michael Lee and Scarlett Thomas, what were they doing here?' I asked casually. 'Hardly their scene. I bet they've gone away to disinfect themselves from the stench of second-hand goods.'

Barney was now so red that it looked as if someone had plunged his head into a pan of boiling water, but he hunched over so a curtain of silky hair covered his burning face and grunted something unintelligible.

'You and Scarlett?' I prompted.

'Er, what about me and Scarlett?' he asked in a strangulated voice.

I shrugged. 'Just saw her checking out the stall when I was trying on dresses. I hope you gave her the hard sell and offloaded that chipped "Rugby players do it with odd-shaped balls" mug that I can't shift.'

'Well, no, I didn't have a chance,' Barney admitted, as if he was confessing to something shameful. 'And that mug is really chipped.'

'True. Very true. Not surprised you didn't get round to it,' I said, cocking my head in what I hoped was an understanding manner. 'You two looked pretty tight. What *were* you talking about?'

Barney flailed his hands. 'Nothing!' he yelped, then realised immediately that 'Nothing' was not a suitable reply. 'We talked about Maths and stuff,' he added.

I'd been sure that there wasn't anything going on with Barney and Scarlett apart from some compound fractions, but Barney's apparent guilt was forcing me to rethink that theory.

I knew I could winkle the truth from Barney in nanoseconds, and that the truth was that Barney had a crush on Scarlett – being easy on the eye and untaxing on the brain, she was considered quite a catch. There was no point in getting upset about it, even though I'd raised him to be better than that, and it really wasn't worth talking about any longer. It was far too boring.

'I got you cake,' I reminded Barney and watched his eyes skitter from side to side as if he wasn't sure whether my abrupt change of subject meant that the topic of Scarlett was over and done with or if it was a sneaky tactic to catch him out.

For once, it wasn't. I handed over a huge slab of cake, which was obscured by a napkin. Barney took it warily.

'Well, thanks,' he muttered, as he uncovered his prize and I watched his face go from deep pink to bedsheet-white. Barney was so white that he was only a couple of shades down from albino. He hated his skin almost as much as he hated his orange hair. At school, the lower years call Barney 'the ginger minger', but Barney's hair *isn't* ginger. It's actually the colour of marmalade, except when the sun is shining and it becomes a living flame, which is why I've forbidden him from dyeing it. He's not a minger either. When his face isn't obscured by a thick fringe, his features are delicate, almost girlish, and his eyes, which were fixed on me imploringly, are pond-green. Barney is the only boy I've ever met whose signature colours are white, orange and green. Most other boys are blue or brown, I thought, and made a mental note to explore this colour theory on my blog later in the week. Then I turned my attention back to Barney, who had puckered up his face and was thrusting the napkin and its contents back at me.

'This is carrot cake!'

I nodded. 'Carrot cake with cream-cheese frosting. Yum.'

'Not yum. This is, like, the anti-yum. I ask you to get me a cake. A CAKE! And you come back with something made out of carrots and cheese. That is not cake,' Barney snapped. 'It's non-cake-food disguised as cake.'

I could only stand and stare. I'd seen Barney petulant before – I was usually responsible for it – but I'd never known him quite so snippy.

'But you eat carrots,' I ventured timidly under the weight of Barney's ferocious scowl. 'I'm sure I've seen you eat carrots.'

'I eat them under duress – I have to have meat or potatoes with them.'

'I'm sorry,' I said and I tried to sound like I meant it. Barney was in a very unpredictable mood and I didn't want to trigger another explosion. 'I'm sorry I sucked at the cake selection. I obviously need to work on that.'

'Well, I suppose it's not your fault,' Barney decided magnanimously. He looked at me from under his fringe, a mere glimmer of a smile just hovering on his lips. 'You do really suck at choosing cakes, but it's good to know you suck at something. I was beginning to wonder.'

'I suck at loads of things,' I assured Barney, as I decided that it was probably safe to stand behind the stall with him. 'Can't turn cartwheels. Never got the hang of German and I don't have strong enough facial muscles to arch an eyebrow.'

'It's genetic,' Barney said. 'But I think you can teach yourself to do it.'

I pushed up my right eyebrow with my fingertip. 'Maybe I should tape my eyebrow up every night and hope that my muscle memory kicks in.'

'I bet there's an instruction guide on the internet,' Barney said eagerly. It was just the kind of obscure, random thing that he liked to research. 'I'll put my Google-fu on it, shall I?'

We were friends again. I mean, boyfriend and girlfriend again. I got Barney a slice of chocolate cake, then spent the rest of the afternoon adding to the list of things I absolutely sucked at, which made him laugh.

It was good. We were cool. Though I wondered why I had to run myself down in order to make Barney feel better about our relationship when I was a card-carrying feminist. Like, seriously. I had the word 'feminist' on my business cards. But for once I took the easy option because I couldn't bear the thought of three hours of Barney moping about. I didn't even yell at him when he spilt Dr Pepper on the 'Adorkable' hot water bottle cover it had taken me ages to knit.

2

I hate Jeane Smith.

I hate her stupid grey hair and her disgusting polyester clothes. I hate how she goes out of her way to make herself look as unattractive as possible but still wants everyone to notice her. She should just wear a T-shirt with 'Everyone! Pay attention to me! Right now!' printed on it.

I hate how everything she says is sarcastic and mean and sounds even more sarcastic and mean because of the flat, toneless way she speaks. As if showing emotion or excitement is way too uncool.

I hate the way she shoved her fugly face into mine and jabbed a finger in my chest to make her point. Though, now I think about it, I'm not sure she did do that, but it's the kind of thing she would probably do.

But mostly I hate her for being so obnoxious and such an out of control bitch that even her boyfriend can't stand to be around her and has to start looking for an out. Especially when that out is my girlfriend.

I knew that Barney fancied Scarlett. It was a given. She was really fit. Really, really fit. Whenever we went into town and got within fifty yards of Topshop she was mobbed on all sides by model agency scouts.

But Scarlett never went to see the agencies because she said she was three inches too short to be a model and she was far too shy. Before we started dating, I thought Scarlett's shyness was sweet. But, after a while, shyness isn't endearing and doesn't make you want to protect someone, it makes you secretly grind your teeth in frustration.

The thing about shyness is that it seems a lot like not trying, the same way that Scarlett wasn't even trying to make our relationship work. I was putting the effort in, calling her every night, thinking of cool things to do on our dates. I bought her presents and helped her set up her BlackBerry and in all ways I was an excellent boyfriend. Whether it's football or A-level Physics or dating, what's the point of doing anything if you're going to do it in a half-arsed way? And I don't want to sound bigheaded but I could go out with pretty much any girl at our school – in fact, any girl at any school in our borough. The fact that I *chose* Scarlett should have given her a huge shot of confidence and she could have shown a little gratitude too.

So when I saw Scarlett and Barney together, it made me furious. All I ever got from Scarlett was a lot of hair-tossing and a few wan smiles but Barney got longing looks and giggling. I couldn't actually hear the giggles but I imagined them as tiny, silver daggers aimed right at my heart and, when I turned my head away, I saw a short, squat, grey-haired girl preening in the mirror.

Jeane Smith is the only person at our school that I've never spoken to. Seriously. I hate labels and cliques and all that bullshit about blanking people 'cause they're not into the same music as you or they're crap at sports. I like that I can get on with everyone and always find some common ground to talk about, even if they're not that cool.

Jeane Smith doesn't talk to anyone, apart from that Barney kid. Everyone talks about her, or about her revolting clothes and the arguments she picks with the teachers in every single one of her classes, but no one talks *to* her because if you try to, you find yourself on the business end of some serious snark and a superior stare.

That was what I got when I tried to explain my suspicions about Barney and Scarlett. About halfway through my first sentence, I realised my mistake, but it was too late. I was committed to having a conversation with her. And I don't know how anyone could manage a dead-eyed stare that also promised unimaginable pain but somehow Jeane had mastered the art. It was as if her retinas had been replaced with laser pointers.

Then she was sticking out her chin and being a bitch, and suddenly whatever whacked-out thing that was going on with Barney and Scarlett didn't matter as much as having the last word.

'Nice dress, by the way,' I said, cocking my head at the horrible multi-coloured mess of a dress that she was wearing, and it was a low blow and completely beneath me, but at least it got Jeane Smith to shut up. But then she smirked and she was one of those people who could make a smirk say a thousand words and none of them good ones.

By the time I'd finished that unpleasant little exchange, Scarlett and Barney had finished their silent flirting. She hurried over to me, her face more animated than I'd ever seen it.